Frank nodded. "I'm ready. Let's do it."

The Multi-Axis Trainer started twisting and turning. The colored lights near Frank's left hand began to blink just as the machine flipped him upside down and reversed the spin direction. He started to get dizzy, and he found it harder and harder to concentrate. His head felt as if it were spinning faster and faster.

"Okay!" he shouted. "I've had enough! Turn it off."

The Multi-Axis Trainer didn't slow down.

"I give up!" Frank yelled. "You win!"

Frank couldn't keep his eyes focused, but he thought he could make out a blurred figure standing next to the controls.

"Shut it down!" Frank shouted. The machine responded by twisting and wrenching Frank around even faster and harder than before.

With growing horror, he realized that he had walked right into a trap . . . and that this fiendish ride was never going to end!

Books in THE HARDY BOYS CASEFILES™ Series

Available from ARCHWAY Paperbacks

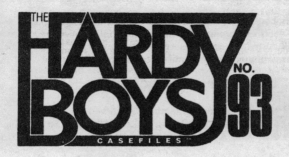

THE HARDY BOYS CASEFILES NO. 93

MISSION: MAYHEM

FRANKLIN W. DIXON

AN ARCHWAY PAPERBACK
Published by POCKET BOOKS
New York   London   Toronto   Sydney   Tokyo   Singapore

This book is a work of fiction. Names, characters, places and incidents are products of the author's imagination or are used fictitiously. Any resemblance to actual events or locales or persons, living or dead, is entirely coincidental.

AN ARCHWAY PAPERBACK *Original*

An Archway Paperback published by
POCKET BOOKS, a division of Simon & Schuster Inc.
1230 Avenue of the Americas, New York, NY 10020

ISBN: 0-671-88204-X

First Archway Paperback printing November 1994

10 9 8 7 6 5 4 3 2 1

Cover art by Brian Kotzky

Printed in the U.S.A.

IL 6+

MISSION:
MAYHEM

Chapter
1

"THIS IS INCREDIBLE," Joe Hardy whispered. "What do all those gizmos do?"

"Shhh," Frank Hardy responded without looking at his brother. His eyes were scanning the bank of computer consoles, bristling with dials, meters, and switches. "They're starting the countdown."

"Coming up on ten," announced one of the technicians speaking into a headset. "T minus ten—nine . . ."

"We are go for main engine start," another technician spoke up. "We have SSME ignition."

"Roger," came a voice from a video monitor on the wall. Frank glanced at the screen and

1

saw a figure in a flight suit strapped into a cockpit, checking off items in a loose-leaf notebook. A pilot sat beside him, monitoring the controls.

"Five—four . . ." the first technician continued calmly.

"We have SRB ignition," a third person at the computer console said.

"Two—one—liftoff!"

Frank watched intently as streams of data lit up the computer screens.

"Shuttle has cleared the tower," someone called out. "Mission control confirms, roll maneuver started."

"Okay," the voice on the video monitor said. "What do we do now?"

A guy in a baseball cap at the far end of the row of computer consoles laughed shortly. "You're the shuttle commander. Don't you know?" he said into his headset microphone. "You're lucky the launch sequence is computerized."

The technician who had called out the countdown grinned. "Thrust looks real good," she said.

Joe looked over at her—a pretty young woman with blond hair, not much older than he was. At seventeen, Joe knew he wasn't ready for a job like this.

"Counting twenty-five seconds," she continued, glancing from a loose-leaf notebook to the computer screen. "Roll maneuver completed."

The technicians continued to call out technical jargon that meant absolutely nothing to Joe.

"Mark one minute, fifty-five seconds."

"Altitude twenty-one nautical miles."

"Coming up on SRB burnout."

"Stand by for solid rocket booster separation."

"Four—three—two—one . . . Uh-oh."

There was a moment of awkward silence during which Frank and Joe silently checked with each other.

"What's going on?" the shuttle commander's nervous voice came over the television speaker. "What's the matter?"

"SRB separation failed," a technician explained into his microphone. "You'll have to disengage the boosters manually."

"What?" the commander blurted out. Joe watched the monitor and saw him flip through the pages of his notebook. "How do we do that?"

"There's a switch here on the console," the pilot's voice remarked through the speaker.

"Keep your hands off those controls!" the shuttle commander snapped, grabbing the pilot's arm as he reached for the switch. "I give the orders here!"

"You'll order us straight down into the ocean if we don't jettison the SRBs!"

In the control room, lights started flashing on the instrument panels.

"Shuttle speed is dropping rapidly!" the blond technician shouted. "It's going to stall out!"

The technician with the baseball cap leaned closer to his computer monitor. His eyes widened as he read the numbers on the screen. "Shuttle is losing altitude!"

"Switch to manual override!" the commander's frantic voice blared from the speaker.

"It's too late," the blond technician moaned. "Ten seconds to impact."

The guy in the baseball cap ripped off his headset and threw it on the ground. The blond whipped through the pages of her manual, desperately searching for some way to save the shuttle. The rest of the ground control crew stared helplessly at their computer screens as the final seconds ticked away.

The deathly silence of the mission control center was finally broken by a voice crackling from the speaker. "Uh, could we try that again?"

A man in a light blue flight suit got up from a computer terminal in the corner, strode up to the bank of controls, and snatched up the discarded headset. "Nope," his gruff voice barked into the microphone. "You're all dead."

Stunned and amazed, the Hardys and a small group of other onlookers followed their tour guide out of the Space and Rocket Center's mission control center into a vast, cluttered space that was like a high-tech warehouse. Teenagers like Frank and Joe—and younger kids, too—were grouped ten or twelve together all around the enormous room. Some sat cross-legged on the floor, listening to young men and women dressed in one-piece blue flight suits. Others were strapped into an assortment of training devices that lifted, twirled, and bounced them around. Tourists in shorts and T-shirts were leaning over a guardrail that separated them from the bustling activity to click snapshots.

Joe's eyes lingered on one contraption that resembled a giant gyroscope at least seven feet high. All at once his attention was drawn to the glum crew filing out of the full-size space shuttle simulator. He recognized the shuttle commander he'd seen on the video screen, now looking utterly dejected.

"That could be you a week from now," the tour guide, a square-jawed young man in one of the academy's blue flight suits, told the group of new trainees. "So shape up and pay attention. You'll need every bit of information we feed you to carry out your own shuttle mission."

The guide had introduced himself during the orientation earlier that morning. He was Steve Swain. Not only would he give the group a tour of the Space Academy's grounds, but he'd be their team leader, too.

Swain's black hair was cropped so short that Joe could see scalp gleaming in the bright fluorescent lights. He was a few inches shorter than either of the Hardys, who were six feet and six one. His dark brown eyes swept over his group with a cool, calculating gaze, then moved down to the clipboard in his hands.

"I've reviewed your enrollment forms," Swain added, "and I've divided you into two six-man teams."

The tall, lanky girl standing next to Joe cleared her throat loudly.

Swain glanced up from his clipboard and offered a grim smile. "Excuse me, Ms. Galewski. I mean six-person teams, of course."

"Thank you, sir," the girl responded, brushing back a strand of brown hair that had escaped from her tight, no-nonsense ponytail.

Swain nodded. "As I was saying, you'll be training in two six-*person* teams. Get to know your teammates. Your lives may depend on them. If you work hard and pay attention, you may get lucky and survive your final mission."

Joe glanced over at his brother. "Welcome to Space Camp," he muttered.

"Space *Academy*," Frank corrected in a whisper.

The difference was important to Frank. Although Space Camp and Space Academy were both part of the U.S. Space and Rocket Center in Huntsville, Alabama, and shared the same facilities and equipment, the Space Camp program for younger kids was mostly space-age amusement rides with lunch breaks.

Space Academy was entirely different. It was as close as a high school student could get to *real* astronaut training. The eight-day course also counted for college credit in science. This fact had helped persuade the Hardys' parents to let Frank and Joe take time off from school to participate in the training program.

After Swain announced the team assignments, he called a lunch break. "You'll eat your meals at the Space Camp cafeteria," he explained, pointing toward a dining area a short distance from the Training Center. Joe noted that several of the long tables were already occupied by other teams as well as tourists from the Space Museum, which was located in the same building.

"After lunch, do we get to try out the training equipment?" Joe asked.

"After lunch we meet in the team room for your first physics class," Swain informed him. "No point in working out on the Five Degrees of Freedom trainer if you don't know the five degrees."

"What did he say?" Joe asked Frank as they joined their teammates in the cafeteria line.

"Five degrees of freedom," Frank explained. "Those are the five directions astronauts can move in space using their Manned Maneuvering Units: forward-backward, side to side, pitch, roll, and yaw. Real astronauts practice moving around on a special training machine. We'll get to use it, too, once we've learned the basics of space physics."

Joe shook his head as he carried his tray to a table where the other team members had already gathered. "Bummer," he said as he sat down next to Maria Galewski, the brown-haired girl who had challenged their team leader earlier. "I thought we'd be flying the shuttle simulator from day one. I didn't know we'd have to learn a bunch of math and science first."

The tall girl with the ponytail gave him a disdainful look. "Isn't that just like a guy," she said. "It takes more than guts to be an astronaut, you know. You have to be educated, too."

Joe scowled. A short girl with frizzy red hair and freckles who sat across from them smiled at him and said, "I have to admit, I wanted to come mostly because of all the cool training equipment, too. You're Joe?" she said, reading the blue-and-white Space Academy ID tag clipped to his shirt. She turned to Frank, who had set his tray down next to hers. "And you're Frank. I remember from the orientation session. I'm Alice Culbert, from Chicago."

"Nice to meet you, Alice," Joe said with a grin. "I'm glad someone agrees with me." He shot a glance at Maria Galewski before turning to a skinny guy seated on the other side of Frank. "I'm sorry," he said, trying to get a look at the guy's ID tag. "What's your name again?"

"Harold. Harold Jenkins." A string of black hair kept falling over his forehead, which he continually flipped back with a jerky twist of his head. He clutched a small appointment book. "I'm his personal assistant," he added, indicating the team member on his left. "I guess you all know who he is."

Joe studied the pair across the table. Harold was all skin and bones and twitches. His companion looked like someone in a magazine ad, with stylishly mussed ash-blond hair, a strong

9

chin with a slight cleft, and warm gray eyes. His fluid movements signaled his cool self-confidence.

The blond teenager flashed a bright white perfect-teeth smile. "I took off my ID tag so word wouldn't get out that I'm here," he explained to Joe and the others. "Otherwise, we'd be drowned in reporters and photographers. I don't want to ruin your training session just because you're on the same team as me."

"Reporters? Photographers?" Alice Culbert leaned past Frank to get a good look at the speaker. "Who are you?"

The teenager's confident smile faltered. "You don't recognize me?" he said in surprise.

Frank and Joe glanced at each other. Joe shrugged.

"Should we?" Frank asked.

"This is Greg Fontana!" Harold Jenkins sputtered. "The star of *Family Troubles*. It was the number-one show on television for four years."

"Oh, that Greg Fontana," Alice said, her face red. She leaned back in her seat. "Sorry— but you don't look much like I remember from the show."

"I understand," Greg told her with a friendly grin. "It was a long time ago, and I was just a kid."

"What are you doing now?" Frank asked, taking a bite of roast beef and gravy.

Greg's smile widened. "I'm working on a new movie. That's why I'm here at Space Academy."

"He's preparing for his role," Harold explained enthusiastically. "This is going to be his comeback. Greg's playing the oldest son of a family marooned on a damaged starship that went off course."

"The movie studio is paying for this training session," Greg added, taking a sip of iced tea. "I get to have fun with you guys this week for free!"

"Must be nice," Maria said a little stiffly. "I waited tables in a pizza joint every day after school for two years to save the money for this course. This isn't playacting to me, and it isn't an amusement park either." She shoved her chair back and stood up without finishing her lunch. "I'm going to be a real astronaut someday." She stared openly at Greg, then at Joe, offering each a thin smile. "I hope you *boys* don't have too much trouble keeping up with me."

"Was it something I said?" Joe asked, checking with the other team members as Maria walked away.

Frank shrugged.

Greg Fontana smiled and stood up. He put

his hands on his hips and stared down at Joe. "The world would be a much better place without all you *boys* around to mess things up."

Joe chuckled. "That's a pretty good imitation of Maria."

"Give me a couple days to work on it," Greg replied with his infectious grin, "and you won't be able to tell us apart."

The rest of the day was full of classes, facts, and figures that made Joe's head spin.

"This is harder than school," he groaned as he lay on his bed in the Space Habitat dormitory that night, staring up at the shiny, corrugated metal ceiling.

Like everything else at Space Academy, the dormitory was designed to put its residents in an astronaut mind-set. Built to look just like NASA's proposed Space Station Habitat, the building consisted of clusters of giant aluminum tubes joined together to form a long, narrow three-story structure. Inside, aluminum stairways and catwalks led to compact sleeping bays. Space Habitat had no windows or bathrooms; it had bubble-shaped "earth-study portholes" and energy-efficient "waste management units."

Frank was sitting on the edge of his bed in the top-floor room they shared with Greg and

Harold. He had to crouch slightly to keep from hitting his head on the ceiling. There was just enough space in the room for six bunks, six lockers, and two built-in desks.

"What did you expect?" Frank responded to Joe as he studied the thick workbook in his lap.

"I don't know," Joe said. "But I sure didn't expect a bunch of physics and chemistry. What was that awful stuff the instructor made us smell?"

"Nitrogen tetroxide," Harold Jenkins answered from one of the desks. "It's one of the fuel components for the shuttle's on-board maneuvering system. It combines with monomethyl hydrazine in a hypergolic reaction."

"That means they ignite on contact," Greg added from his lower bunk.

"I think I got all that," Joe said. "But why did the instructor make us take a whiff of that junk?"

"Because nitrogen tetroxide is highly toxic and corrosive when exposed to moisture," Frank told him. "If you smell it inside the shuttle, then you know you've got a serious problem."

"Terrific," Joe muttered. "What are you supposed to do about it when you're a few hundred miles above earth?"

"Maybe we'll learn that tomorrow," Frank

replied, shutting his workbook with a sigh. "I'm beat. As far as I'm concerned, it's lights out."

As soon as his head hit his pillow, Joe fell into a deep sleep. He knew he had to get up early in the morning, but it seemed as if he had barely closed his eyes when someone started shaking him.

"Go away," Joe mumbled.

"Get up!" Frank yelled, dragging his brother out of bed. "Now!"

"Okay, okay. What'd I do already?" Joe muttered, starting to yawn. His yawn was cut off as he began to cough. "Smoke!" he rasped, his eyes opening wide. "What's going on?"

"The room's on fire!" Frank shouted, hauling Joe to his feet. "Get up! We've got to get out!"

Joe saw that the door to the dorm room was in flames. Smoke filled the tiny sleep bay. There was no way they could get past the fire to the catwalk. They were trapped!

eted on the smoldering doorway of their room, "but I plan to find out."

The Hardys spent the rest of the night on cots in a spare room. After a few fitful hours of sleep, Frank and Joe got ready to face the challenges of their second day at Space Academy.

The Training Center was just a short walk from the Habitat dormitory, just past Shuttle Park. The park was a circular concrete plaza, dominated by the towering form of the space shuttle *Pathfinder,* riding on top of its huge external fuel tank with two solid rocket boosters strapped to the side.

As Frank and Joe passed through the shadow of the *Pathfinder,* they ran into a small crowd of reporters and photographers. Beyond the huddle of newspeople jostling for position was Greg Fontana, pushing away a microphone being thrust into his face.

"After being a television star, how does it feel to be a hero?" one of the reporters asked.

"I'm not a hero," Greg replied, surprised. "Anybody could have done what I did."

"Well, not anybody," Harold Jenkins spoke up, clutching the nearest microphone. "But self-sacrifice means nothing to Greg."

"Give me a break," Frank heard someone mutter behind him.

Frank turned to see a man in a corduroy sports jacket scribbling in a notebook. The man was a few inches shorter than Frank, and he had curly brown hair.

He glanced up from his notebook and met Frank's gaze. "I'm sorry," he said dryly. "I'll try to keep my editorial comments to myself."

"Are you a reporter?" Frank asked.

The man nodded. "I'm writing an article on Fontana for *Profiles* magazine."

"Wow," Joe said, joining the conversation, "I didn't think a small fire in Huntsville, Alabama, would rate coverage from a national magazine."

The man chuckled, his alert, dark eyes flicking to Joe. "It doesn't. I'm doing a piece on Fontana's comeback in show business. I got this assignment a few weeks ago. I was right across the street at the hotel when the fire broke out, but I slept right through it.

"My name's Mike Baron," he continued. "I already know quite a lot about Fontana, and I'm having a hard time believing he put out that fire all by himself."

"Believe it," Joe said. "We were there. We saw the whole thing."

The reporter raised his eyebrows. "Really? Let me get your names down, and then tell me the whole story."

Frank and Joe spent a few minutes talking

with the reporter. After that they grabbed a quick breakfast at the cafeteria. Then they had to endure an hour of brutal calisthenics that met all of Joe's expectations for the rigors of army boot camp. The master of ceremonies for the torture session was Steve Swain.

The exercise period was followed by a class in which Joe discovered that flying the shuttle wouldn't be quite as easy as driving the Hardys' van back home. With over a hundred controls and displays on the flight deck, Joe figured he'd be lucky to figure out what *half* of them did in one short week.

While Joe barely managed to keep up with the heavy flow of information, Frank thrived on the technical challenge. He had done his homework the night before—and so had Maria Galewski. Every time the instructor asked a question, they were both ready with the answer. Frank knew that his brother would weigh only thirty pounds on the moon, and Maria pointed out that Frank could graduate from college in the time it would take to travel to Mars.

No matter who answered the question, Maria always had some minor correction or extra tidbit of information to toss in. She even corrected the instructor a few times. Frank noticed that Steve Swain didn't like being corrected.

* * *

The team sat together for lunch in the cafeteria. "I'm still sore from our workout this morning," Joe said as he sat down. "Swain is a regular drill sergeant."

"Actually, he's a captain in the air force," Maria responded. "He's also an astronaut."

"What's he doing at Space Academy?" Alice Culbert asked.

"People from Nasa help develop the courses and give lectures here," Harold Jenkins pointed out. He turned to Maria. "But I didn't know any active astronauts were working as team leaders."

"Are you sure Swain is an astronaut?" Frank asked Maria.

"Of course I'm sure. I know the names of all the astronauts in the space program," Maria replied. "I get every newsletter and brochure that NASA sends out."

"You're really serious about training to be an astronaut, aren't you?" Frank asked.

"That's right," Maria said. She glanced at her watch and stood up. "I'm going to hit the books for a while. I'll meet you guys at the wall at thirteen hundred hours."

"What did she mean by that?" Joe asked as Maria walked away.

"Check the schedule," Alice answered. "We have a training session on the Zero 'G' Wall at one o'clock this afternoon."

"Thanks for the translation," Joe said. "What's the Zero 'G' Wall?"

Alice grinned. "You'll see. It should be fun."

Joe sighed. "I sure hope so."

"I think I'm going to take a walk outside and get some fresh air," Greg said.

"I'll go with you," Harold offered, starting to rise.

"Take it easy, Harold. You don't have to shadow me," Greg said mildly, waving his assistant to sit back down. "I'll meet you at the wall at one. Don't worry. I promise I won't be late."

Even though Frank and Joe got to the Zero "G" Wall a few minutes early, Greg and Maria were already there. While they waited for their instructor, Frank checked out the "wall," which was actually a thirty-foot high black metal framework. Frank had read all the brochures about Space Academy, and he knew the nearby two-story water tank was used to simulate weightless conditions in space. He also knew the pair of harnesses that dangled on cables in front of the Zero "G" Wall were designed to do the same thing.

When Steve Swain arrived, the instructor confirmed what Frank had already figured out.

"If you ever wondered what it would be like

to repair something in outer space," Swain said, grasping one of the slightly swaying harnesses, "here's your chance to find out."

"I wonder how the guys at the video store repair my VCR," Greg Fontana quipped. "And they do it right here on earth. But for the rates they charge," he added with a grin at his teammates, "they should be doing it in outer space."

Swain turned to Greg. "You'll be our first volunteer," he said, pointing at the actor. "Now we need somebody to work with you."

Greg grabbed Joe's arm and dragged him toward the wall. "My friend here is eager to give it a try," Greg proclaimed.

Swain glanced down at his clipboard. "Your friend is Joe Hardy, right?"

"Right," Joe said, "but I—"

"Put a lid on it." Swain cut him off. "You'll have to learn to do this sooner or later. You might as well go first and set a good example."

"Hold it," Greg cut in as Swain started to buckle Joe into one of the harnesses. "Would you mind if I use that one? I'd feel more comfortable on the right side."

Swain sighed with impatience. "Is that okay with you?" he asked Joe.

Joe shrugged. "Sure. Why not?"

"As you can see," Swain announced to the class when Joe and Greg were buckled in, "the harness is attached to a cable, and the cable runs through a series of overhead pulleys. And as our two volunteers can tell you, the harness neutralizes their weight."

"That's true," Joe agreed, bobbing slightly in the harness, his toes lightly grazing the floor. "Are we going to do anything besides just hang here?"

Swain took a short plastic pole out of a box on the floor. "We're going to simulate an outer space repair job by building a small addition onto the wall with the poles and connectors I have here. You two climb up about ten feet, and I'll hand you the poles one at a time."

"That's all?" Joe said, relieved. "We could do that without safety harnesses."

The instructor smiled. "Then this should be easy for you." He looked over at Greg. "Are you ready?"

Greg nodded and gave the thumbs-up signal.

"Okay," Swain said. "Get going."

Joe grabbed a rung and started to climb. With the harness supporting his entire weight, he easily glided twenty-five feet up the wall. He grabbed for a rung a few feet over his head, missed, and kept floating upward.

There were a few gasps from the other campers, followed by scattered laughter as Joe jerked around and tried to snatch another rung with his outstretched hand. He only succeeded in twisting himself around, and he continued to float to the top of the wall—a full thirty feet above the floor.

"It's easy to move around in space," Joe heard Swain tell the class far below. "The tricky part is *stopping*."

"Hang in there," Greg called up to Joe. "I'll come up and give you a hand."

"Thanks," Joe grumbled from his position high above the floor. He kept squirming in the harness, trying to twist back around to face the wall. He wanted to get himself out of this mess without being rescued.

Just then Joe felt something give way in the shoulder harness. There was a soft metallic *snick,* and Joe pitched forward, his head falling below his feet. Then he began to slide out of the harness. He fell too quickly to catch at the harness with his hands. Only his legs, getting caught in the rigging, held him. "Whoa!" he yelled, trying to regain his balance.

Joe dangled helplessly upside-down two stories off the ground. Somebody screamed, and nobody was laughing anymore. Joe felt incredibly stupid and a little scared.

Then he felt his legs slipping out of the harness. Joe glanced down at the horror-struck crowd spinning far below. Maria was staring up at him, her fists clenched. Alice also watched round-eyed, a hand covering her mouth. Any second now, Joe realized, he was going to fall. He wasn't going to be weightless, though, when his head smashed into the ground.

Chapter

3

JOE FELT his legs slipping through the harness. He tried to grab a rung of the Zero "G" Wall, but the harness hung too far out. Joe could only flail his arms wildly.

One leg slid out of the rigging. Now just one foot remained hooked in the harness. Joe took another desperate swipe at the metal framework. His foot popped out of the harness, and Joe started to plummet.

Something clamped onto Joe's ankle and held him suspended in the air. Joe twisted his head around and looked up at Greg Fontana. He was hanging on to a rung of the wall with one hand, and his other hand was wrapped tightly around Joe's ankle.

"Where do you think you're going?" Greg grunted through clenched teeth as he struggled to maintain his grip on Joe's leg. "We've got work to do up here."

Down on the floor, Frank had rushed over to help break Joe's fall, and now he eased him down as Swain lowered Greg's harness.

"What happened?" Frank asked his brother as the other campers looked on, dumbstruck.

Joe shook his head. "I don't know. Something snapped in my harness."

"Nothing like this has ever happened," Swain said. He gave Joe and Greg a sharp look. "And it probably wouldn't have happened if you two clowns had been a little more careful."

Joe stared at the instructor. "You're kidding, right? That contraption almost gets me killed, and it's *my* fault?"

"You weren't in any real danger," Swain responded in a dismissive tone. "We were right here and would have caught you."

"Not in any danger?" Harold reacted indignantly. "It looked dangerous to me. What if Greg had been in that harness? He could have been killed!"

"I think we're all a little on edge after that scare," Frank interjected, trying to defuse the situation.

27

"I'll say," Alice Culbert agreed. "My heart's still going a mile a minute."

Swain nodded slowly. "You're right. Let's take a break and meet back here in a half hour. That should give me enough time to hook up a new harness."

"I'd like to take a look at the broken one," Frank said.

"I'll take care of it," Swain said sharply. "And the sooner you get out of here, the sooner I'll be able to fix the problem."

"I don't think Swain likes us very much," Joe observed as they walked back to the Space Habitat.

"I don't think he likes *anybody* very much," Greg said.

"I think we're lucky to have an astronaut for our instructor," Maria spoke up. She looked over at Frank. "What did you say that got him so upset?"

"I just wanted to check out the broken harness," Frank answered.

"Why would you want to do that?" Alice Culbert asked.

"Frank has a suspicious mind," Joe responded. "He hates accidents."

"Some accidents turn out to be something else entirely," Frank said.

Greg chuckled. "You sound like a character in a detective novel."

"Don't laugh," Joe said. "Our father is a private investigator, and we've cracked a few cases ourselves."

Greg rolled his eyes. "Are you guys going to spend the rest of the week searching for spies under our beds?"

"I just hope we have some beds to look under," Frank replied with a smile. "I don't want to spend another night on one of those Stone Age cots."

"I don't think the fire damage was too bad," Harold Jenkins said. "The room may even be fixed up by now."

"Let's find out," Frank said.

The two girls headed off for their floor of Space Habitat, and the four boys climbed the stairs to the top floor.

They had to squeeze past a pair of workmen who were fitting a new door on the dorm room. Inside, Frank could see that Harold was right. The fire had seemed incredibly intense in the middle of the night—but in the light of day there was very little real damage.

"Have you ever been in a restaurant where they serve those fancy flaming desserts?" Frank mused out loud as he surveyed the room.

Joe glanced at his brother. "Are you just

making idle conversation or is this leading somewhere?"

"I was wondering the same thing," Greg remarked.

"The dessert doesn't burn," Frank explained. "It doesn't even get hot. The flame is from alcohol poured over the dessert. If you blow out the flame before all the alcohol burns off, the fire never touches anything else."

"You sound like you know a lot about fires," a man with a deep drawl spoke up behind him.

Frank spun around to face a balding man in a rumpled brown suit standing in the doorway.

"I know a lot about a lot of things," Frank said simply.

"He reads a lot," Joe added.

The man walked into the room. "What are you boys doing here?"

"This is our room," Frank said. "What are *you* doing here?"

The man reached into the jacket of his suit and pulled out an ID card and badge. "I'm Detective Walsh, Huntsville Police." He strolled over to the row of lockers that had escaped the fire unscathed. "Is there anything in here?"

"I sure hope so," Joe said. "If the rest of my clothes aren't in my locker, this outfit I'm wearing is going to smell pretty rank by the end of the week."

The detective smiled thinly. "Would you mind if I take a look inside?"

"Hey, wait a minute," Harold said. "What's going on here? Why do you want to search our lockers? We haven't done anything wrong."

"Somebody did," Detective Walsh said.

"Did what?" Joe responded.

"The fire wasn't an accident," Frank answered. "It was arson."

The detective raised his eyebrows. "Who told you that?"

"The evidence told me," Frank replied. "The door and half the wall next to it were covered in flames last night, but look at the wall now. The fire barely touched it."

Joe frowned. "I don't get it."

"The wall never caught on fire," Frank explained. "What we saw burning was some kind of flammable liquid that was splashed on the wall and the door."

"Very good," the police detective said. "The preliminary lab tests indicate as much."

Greg Fontana shook his head slowly. "Now I'm the one who doesn't get it. Why would somebody deliberately set our room on fire?"

Detective Walsh shrugged. "It's my job to find out." He nodded toward the lockers. "And if you boys give me permission to search your lockers, it would make my job a lot easier."

Nobody objected, and the search didn't reveal anything unusual or suspicious.

"Did you really think you'd find anything?" Joe asked the detective as he was leaving. "What kind of arsonist would leave evidence in his locker?"

"An *amateur* arsonist," Walsh replied. "I hope this whole incident was just a stupid prank that got out of control. If not, we're dealing with a very sick, very dangerous character."

The team met back at the Training Center later that afternoon when everybody got a turn on the Zero "G" Wall. Frank was teamed with Maria, and she proved to be as adept on the wall as she was in the classroom.

When the session was over, Frank and Joe hung around the Training Center. The area was still full of campers, with a small cluster of sightseers watching from behind the wall.

"I didn't know all the training exercises would be live performances for an audience of gawkers," Joe remarked.

"The U.S. Space and Rocket Center is open to the public," Frank noted as they walked around, checking out the equipment. "Space Academy is right in the middle of the center. So we have to put up with a few curious tourists."

He wandered behind a full-size mock-up of the Spacelab module and stopped in front of a door in the back wall of the Training Center marked Maintenance Area, Staff Only. Frank hoped this would be the place to begin his search for clues. He pushed open the door and motioned for Joe to follow him. The maintenance area turned out to be one cluttered room full of scattered tools and equipment that was in the process of being repaired.

Frank heard footsteps scuffing across the floor. He ducked behind a tool cabinet and dragged his brother down beside him. He peered around the side of the cabinet and spotted a man in grease-stained coveralls pushing a hand cart at the far end of the room. Frank and Joe shrank back in the shadows as the man moved toward them. He walked right past their hiding spot, opened the door, and hauled the cart out into the Training Center.

After the door swung shut behind him, the Hardys crawled out from behind the cabinet.

"What are we doing in here?" Joe asked in a low voice, barely above a whisper.

"Looking for something," Frank answered as his alert brown eyes scanned the room.

"Could you narrow that down a little for me?" Joe responded.

Frank nodded toward a workbench. "I think I found the place to start."

Joe spotted his harness from the Zero "G" Wall sprawled out on the workbench.

"If we're lucky, nobody has touched it yet," Frank said, leaning over to inspect the harness closely.

"I don't think this is a good week to test our luck," Joe said. "First we almost got barbecued in our room, and then I found out what happens when bungee jumpers buy cheap gear."

Frank slowly turned the harness over, carefully examining both sides of the straps and buckles. "Quite a coincidence, don't you think? Two near-fatal incidents, and we were right in the middle of the action both times."

"Come on, Frank. You don't really think someone here is trying to hurt us, do you?" Joe asked.

"I don't know why anybody would be after us, but we do know the fire wasn't an accident," Frank pointed out. He pulled a penlight out of his pocket and aimed the narrow beam into one of the slots on the large buckle where all the shoulder and leg straps snapped together in the middle of the harness. "See if you can find a pair of tweezers," he told his brother as he squinted inside the buckle.

Joe sifted through the assorted tools piled on the workbench. "How about a screwdriver?" he asked.

Frank glanced at the long, thin screwdriver. "That should do the trick."

Frank slipped the blade of the screwdriver into the slot, worked it around for a minute, and then pried it back out slowly.

"There it is," he said, plucking something off the tip of the blade and holding it out to his brother. It was about the size of a dollar bill torn in half.

"This is what you were looking for?" Joe asked, staring into Frank's open palm. "A scrap of cloth?"

As the words left his mouth, Joe realized how dangerous the seemingly harmless piece of fabric could be in the wrong place. "That's all it would take to prevent the shoulder strap from fully locking into the buckle, right?" he said.

Frank nodded.

"How did it get in there?"

"Would you feel better if I told you it was probably an accident?" Frank responded.

Joe shook his head. "I doubt it."

"Good," Frank said grimly. "Then I won't have to lie. Whoever stuck this cloth in your harness knew what he was doing. And what he was doing almost got you killed, Joe."

Chapter

4

"WE CAN'T BE SURE the cloth didn't get wedged into the buckle accidentally," Joe protested.

"No," Frank admitted. "We can't prove anything either way—not yet, anyway. Also, we don't know who might have done it or why."

Joe took the strip of blue fabric from his brother. "This is the same color as the flight suits all the instructors wear," he noted.

"That's not much of a lead," Frank replied. "Half the campers have the same outfits. Those flight suits are the hottest item in the gift shop."

Joe nodded. "You're right. Maria was wearing one today. I bought one, too."

Frank plucked the swatch of material out of Joe's hand and put it in his pocket. "We'd better get moving before somebody finds us in here."

The Hardys slipped out of the maintenance area and into the Training Center. A few sessions were still going on. Joe gazed up at a girl in a spacesuit strapped into a contraption that looked like a cross between a robot warrior's backpack and a lounge chair from the future. The boxy white contraption was dangling a good thirty feet off the floor, attached to a jointed crane device that rose up out of the cargo bay of the shuttle simulator.

Joe had already learned in class that the contraption that held the white machine was called a Manned Maneuvering Unit. Like most of the equipment with long names in the program, everybody referred to it by its initials—MMU. This was the Five Degrees of Freedom trainer that Steve Swain had mentioned on their initiation tour.

"Maybe we're not the targets," Frank said, bringing Joe's attention back to their case.

Joe stared at his brother. "Who else could it be? It was our room that got torched, and I was the one in the sabotaged harness."

"We weren't the only guys in that room," Frank pointed out. "And there's something that bothers me about what happened to you."

37

"You mean, *besides* the fact that I almost got my brains smashed?" Joe grumbled.

Frank struggled to hold back a grin. "You may not have noticed any difference."

"Very funny," Joe muttered. He glanced at the Zero "G" Wall. "Wait a minute. Who knew I would be the first person to get into that harness?"

"That's what bothers me," Frank said. "But I'm working on it." He replayed the events in his head. "Nobody on the team knew who would go first. I don't think Swain even knew. It didn't seem like he had a definite plan. He didn't even pick you."

"No," Joe responded, "but he did pick Greg."

Frank's eyes widened. "And you guys switched harnesses at the last second."

Joe nodded. "And Greg was in the same dorm room with us."

The Hardys wandered outside into the cool autumn afternoon.

"But why would Swain be out to get Greg?" Joe asked when they were clear of the building and nobody else was in earshot.

"I'm working on that, too," Frank said.

Frank mulled over the facts. It didn't take long; they didn't have a lot of information to work with. "We need to find out more about Swain," he concluded.

When they reached the dormitory, they headed for the counselors' lounge on Space Habitat's first floor. A counselor not much older than Frank—twenty at the most—was sitting on a couch, thumbing through a magazine.

Frank hoped the guy's age would work in their favor. Somebody close in age might be a little easier to pump for information. Then again, the counselor might pull rank and order the Hardys out of the staff lounge before they had a chance to speak.

Frank cleared his throat.

The counselor turned his head. "Hi," he said, getting up off the couch. "Can I do something for you guys?"

At least he didn't call them *boys*. Frank took that as a good sign.

"We're looking for our team leader," Frank said. "We thought he might be here."

"It's just me right now," the young counselor said. 'You could leave a message, though, if you want. What's your team leader's name?"

"Steve Swain," Frank replied.

"Too bad," the counselor said with a soft chuckle. "Swain's a real hard case."

"Well, I don't think he's out to win any popularity contests," Frank said.

"That's a whopper of an understatement," the counselor responded. "More than a few

39

campers have tried to get reassigned after a few days with Swain."

Frank acted surprised. "I don't believe it. He isn't that bad."

"That's not all," the counselor persisted, lowering his voice. "I've got a friend who works in administration, and she says Swain's file is full of complaints from campers and their parents. The guy treats kids like army recruits."

"Some people will complain about anything," Frank observed. "Just because Swain pushes a little too hard doesn't make him a bad guy."

The instructor snorted. "Tell that to the kid who almost drowned in the underwater training tank. He said Swain poked a hole in his air hose to simulate an air leak during a space walk."

Frank and Joe glanced at each other.

"How could he get away with a stunt like that?" Joe reacted hotly.

"Hold on a second," Frank said. "Was there any proof?" he asked the instructor.

The young man in the blue flight suit shook his head. "No, and Swain denied the whole thing."

"Okay," Frank said, "so all we know for sure is that Swain has a reputation for being a little too gung ho."

"Way too gung ho," Joe amended.

Frank shot his brother a sharp look. Joe's opinion he could get anytime. Frank was trying to get the dirt on their instructor by defending Swain. He hoped Joe would get the hint and either get with the program or stop talking.

"Well," Frank said evenly after a brief silence, "I still think we're pretty lucky to have a real astronaut training us."

*"Ex-*astronaut," the counselor responded. "NASA cut Swain from the shuttle program two days ago because of a minor medical problem. That's why he was here in the first place. He was on extended leave from the program while his condition was being monitored and evaluated. It's nothing serious—slightly elevated blood pressure—but anything short of perfect isn't good enough for shuttle pilots.

"I don't know about you guys," he added, "but I wouldn't want to be anywhere near Swain for the next few weeks. I heard he punched a hole in the office wall when he got the news. He's definitely not happy, and he'll probably do his best to make sure you aren't either."

After dinner that night the Hardys' team watched a film in the giant-screened Space-Dome movie theater. The film, called *Speed,* informed them that going six or seven miles an hour on a bicycle was considered a big deal in the early eighteenth century. Mike Baron, the reporter, tagged along, still working on his story about Greg Fontana.

Joe noticed that every time Baron asked Greg a question, Harold Jenkins was ready with the answer. Joe guessed that dealing with reporters' boring questions must be one of the assistant's major duties.

After the long, eventful day, Joe was looking forward to a long, uneventful night. He fell asleep a few seconds after his head hit his pillow. The faint odor of smoke that still lingered in the dorm room didn't faze him at all. He was too tired to care.

The only thing that disturbed Joe's sleep was the unwelcome arrival of morning. The only thing that got him out of bed was Frank's insistent prodding.

"Hurry up," Frank urged as Joe stumbled out of bed and moved around for his clothes. "We've only got a few minutes to grab some breakfast before the morning exercise period."

"Not again," Joe groaned. "We did enough calisthenics yesterday to last a month."

"Come on," Greg Fontana chided as the four campers filed out of the dorm room and headed downstairs. "A little exercise never hurt anyone."

"How would you know?" Joe responded. "You weren't even there yesterday."

"That wasn't my fault," Greg said. "I was stuck with those reporters. I guess it was a slow news day in Huntsville."

By the time the Hardys, Harold, and Greg arrived at the cafeteria, their teammates, Maria and Alice, were already returning their trays. Alice waved at the Hardys.

"Better hurry up, boys," Maria said. "NASA doesn't approve of latecomers."

"She's right," Harold moaned, glancing nervously at his watch. He followed Greg, Frank, and Joe to the line. "We're going to be late."

"Relax," Greg said, reaching for a glass of orange juice. "What's Swain going to do if we're a few minutes late? Kill us?"

"That's a distinct possibility," Joe muttered under his breath to Frank.

"You're late!" Swain barked sharply, squinting to focus on the Hardys and their two teammates.

Greg smiled and shrugged. "We slept late this morning. You know how it—"

"Didn't you learn *anything* from that mission you watched the first day?" Swain snapped. "You can't be late when you're piloting a vehicle that's hurtling through space at over seventeen thousand miles per hour. You can't be late when mere seconds could mean the difference between life and death for your entire crew." He gestured at Alice and Maria, who were standing with the other Space Academy team. "And you can't be late for any of my classes! Now get down on the ground and give me fifty push-ups!"

"Gee," Greg responded glibly, "I don't think I can do that many."

A cold grin crept across the instructor's face. "If that's too tough, get out on the track and do ten laps."

"That's two miles," Harold spluttered. "Greg has asthma! He can't run that far!"

Greg put his hand on his assistant's shoulder. "It's okay, Harold. I can handle it."

"You'd better be able to handle it," Swain said tersely. "Because if you can't, you're out of the program."

"If you don't mind," Frank spoke up, "we'll go with Greg."

Swain gestured to the running track. "Be my guest."

Frank, Joe, and Greg started jogging around the wide oval track at an easy pace.

"You've got twelve minutes!" Swain called out. "I want you to remember this workout!"

"Twelve minutes!" Joe exclaimed, glancing over at his brother. "That's a mile in six minutes!"

"We'd better pick up the pace then," Greg panted.

"Are you sure you can make it?" Frank asked him.

"I don't have much of a choice," Greg replied.

Frank kept an eye on Greg as they ran around the track. After the first three laps, the actor was sucking in air in labored gasps.

"You don't have to do this," Frank told him. "Swain can't kick you out of the program."

"That's not the point," Greg wheezed. "If I don't tough it out, Swain will treat me like a wimp for the rest of the course."

Joe shook his head. "This is crazy."

"Don't worry," Greg huffed. "I feel better than I sound."

"You don't *look* very good either," Joe noted. "You're as white as a—"

Greg suddenly clutched at his chest, pain etched on his deathly pale face. He staggered forward one more step before crumpling to the ground in a lifeless heap.

Chapter

5

FRANK AND JOE rushed over and knelt down
next to Greg where he lay sprawled facedown.

"Help me turn him over," Frank told his
brother.

"Should we give him CPR?" Joe asked as
they rolled the actor onto his back. Joe gasped
when he saw the sickly bluish flush that covered Greg's face. He glanced at his brother.
"Is he dead?"

Frank put two fingers against the side of
Greg's neck to feel for a pulse. Before he
could answer Joe's question, the body shook
with a sudden convulsion. The chest heaved,
and a raspy wheeze rose from Greg's throat as
his lungs hungrily gulped air.

The blue tinge faded, and his eyes fluttered open. "What are you guys staring at?" Greg croaked in a hoarse whisper. He gave the Hardys a weak smile. "You look like you just saw a dead body or something."

"Something like that," Joe responded with a sigh of relief.

The rest of the class had picked up on what was happening and crowded around as Frank and Joe helped Greg stand up.

Harold Jenkins shoved his way to the front and jostled Frank aside. Frank backed off and let the scrawny kid put a protective arm around the actor.

"Everybody clear out of the way!" Harold shouted in a shrill voice. "I have to get Greg to the first aid station!"

"I'm okay," Greg insisted, pulling away from his assistant. His eyes found Steve Swain in the small crowd. "Just give me a minute to catch my breath, and I'll finish the two miles."

"Forget it," the instructor said gruffly. "You gave it your best shot, and that's all I expect." He turned to the cluster of campers. "That's all I expect from any of you. Give it your best and don't give up. Now hit the showers. Class in thirty minutes."

He threw his next remark back at Greg and the Hardys: "Try not to be late."

Maria Galewski walked beside Greg as he made his way off the track with the Hardys.

"You should keep yourself in better shape," she said bluntly. "If you can't keep up, maybe you should drop out."

Harold Jenkins whirled and glared at her. "You're just jealous of Greg!" he snapped.

Maria reacted with a short, startled laugh. "Why would I be jealous of him?"

"Because you wanted to be the mission commander," Harold told her, "but Greg's got that assignment."

"What are you talking about?" Joe asked. "Swain hasn't announced any mission assignments yet."

"Didn't anybody tell you?" Maria responded bitterly. "Mr. Hollywood pulled a few strings to make sure he'd get the top spot. He had the commander's job locked before he even showed up for the first class."

"It wasn't my idea," Greg said defensively as Maria walked away. He turned to the Hardys. "My agent and the movie studio thought it would be good publicity."

"I think you're getting too much attention already," Frank said. "But I don't think it's the kind you want."

The Hardys told the actor what they had uncovered about the sabotaged harness and Steve Swain.

"If anybody around here is jealous of you," Joe concluded, "I'd put Swain at the top of the list. His career just went down the tubes, and then you show up with reporters following you around and movie moguls pulling strings for you."

"We know the guy has a short fuse," Frank added. "You may have set him off just by being here."

Greg shook his head slowly. "There you go again, sounding like a couple of B-movie gumshoes. Nobody is out to get me, and I don't need you to be my bodyguards. Stop looking for bombs under the car and try to enjoy the ride."

To get to their class, the Hardys went through the Space Museum. Everything at the Space and Rocket Center was part of one big, sprawling complex, and the only way to get from the Training Center to the lecture room was through the museum.

The museum was full of exhibits on the history of space exploration. Frank and Joe had spent a few hours wandering around the museum on the first day. Glancing at some of the early efforts of the space program now, Frank realized the flight deck of the shuttle must seem like a luxury hotel suite to the astronauts who endured the sparse, cramped quarters of the lunar landing module or a Gemini capsule.

In the lecture room was a white-haired man standing next to Steve Swain at the front of the room. Frank noted that he wasn't wearing a blue flight suit as the Space Academy instructors did. He had on the uniform of an air force colonel.

"We have a special guest today," Swain announced. "This is Colonel Perry Housman. He's flown three shuttle missions himself, one as pilot and two as commander. What he doesn't know about the space shuttle isn't worth knowing. So listen up!"

"I'm glad to have this opportunity to talk to you," the man in the air force uniform told the class. He took a pointer off the lectern and tapped a large schematic drawing of the shuttle on the wall. "By now, you've probably learned that the shuttle is a very complex bird."

Colonel Housman paused and scanned the faces of the campers. "Have any of you ever flown an airplane?"

Frank and Joe raised their hands, and a few other hands went up, too. To Frank's surprise, Maria Galewski's hand was one of them.

"Compared to piloting the shuttle," the colonel continued, "flying an airplane is easier than riding a tricycle. Have any of you ever dead-stick landed a plane without engine power?"

Frank's hand was the only one that went up this time.

Colonel Housman's blue eyes focused on Frank. "What's your name, son?"

"Frank Hardy, sir."

"Well, Frank, imagine what it would be like to dead-stick land a hundred-ton brick at two hundred fifty miles per hour. That's a *normal* shuttle landing when everything goes perfectly according to plan.

"There is *zero* margin for error on a shuttle flight. That's why the shuttle has three separate computer systems and five on-board computers. You can't fly the thing by yourself, but you can't rely on the machines to do all the work either. If anything goes wrong, the commander depends on his crew to work as a team to bring them all down safely.

"That's what it's all about," Colonel Housman concluded. "Teamwork."

After Housman's brief talk, Swain launched into a demanding lecture on the physics and chemistry of the shuttle's propulsion system. Joe was relieved that Frank and Maria were ready with an answer every time the instructor fired off a question, because he got lost right after the part about how the liquid hydrogen fuel in the external tank is stored at the frigid temperature of *minus* 423 degrees but burns at over six thousand degrees when combined with liquid oxygen.

After the lunch break Swain took the class on a tour of Rocket Park, right outside the Space and Rocket Center complex. Mike Baron, the reporter, tagged along once again, bringing a camera and snapping pictures everywhere, just like half the tourists in the park. Unlike the tourists, Joe noted, Baron's camera was a large professional model with a fat, protruding zoom lens that must have weighed about twenty pounds. Baron wasn't taking snapshots of the rockets; his subject was only Greg Fontana.

Swain led the campers through a forest of spacecraft that spanned more than thirty years of the space program. "This is the Mercury Redstone," Swain told the campers, stopping at a slender white rocket with stubby fins at the bottom.

He pointed to a sooty black tapered capsule perched on the top of the rocket, almost a hundred feet off the ground. "Alan Shepard rode in a capsule like that on a fifteen-minute ride that launched the space program. That was way back in 1961. A year later John Glenn blasted off on top of another Redstone and orbited the planet three times.

"Of course, they weren't the first Americans in space," he added. "Our first astronauts were a couple of monkeys named Able and Miss Baker."

All of the gruffness disappeared from Swain's voice when he talked with reverence about space flight. Joe thought he caught a glimpse of the real man under the tough shell, and he also felt the tug of the ex-astronaut's dream to explore that final frontier.

Swain took the class over to a towering rocket that rose up over two hundred feet in the middle of the park. "This is the Saturn 1, Block 2, the second rocket in the family that spawned the Saturn 5, the booster that launched Neil Armstrong and crew to the moon in 1969.

"As you can see," he added, nodding to a scaffolding that rose about fifty feet up the side of the rocket, "these babies still require a lot of maintenance even when they don't go anywhere."

Joe watched Greg Fontana standing near the scaffolding, taking a close look at one of the rocket's broad tail fins.

Joe walked over to see what Greg found so interesting. As he neared the scaffolding, he heard a hollow *clunk* overhead. He looked up and saw a dark object bounce off one of the scaffold's metal struts. It tumbled down a few feet and clattered off another strut with a ringing *thunk*. Then it plummeted straight down off the side of scaffolding.

Joe didn't need a computer to plot the falling object's trajectory. It was plunging down on a direct collision course with Greg's skull!

Chapter

6

GREG, OBLIVIOUS to the danger overhead, was still standing right under the plummeting object.

Joe knew there was no time for a warning and threw himself across the pavement at the startled actor. Joe smashed into Greg with a flying tackle, driving his shoulder into Greg's stomach.

The force of the blow lifted Greg off the ground. He flew backward with Joe's arms wrapped around his waist. They hit the ground hard. Joe kept a tight grip on Greg and twisted his body with a sharp jerk. Together the two interlocked bodies rolled under the huge engines of the Saturn rocket.

Behind them, something crashed into the cement with a shattering *crack*.

Greg pushed Joe off him and staggered to his feet. "Are you crazy?" he gasped. "You could have killed me!"

Joe pointed to the chunk of metal that smacked into the pavement right where Greg had been standing. "*That* could have killed you."

Joe raised his eyes and saw a figure scrambling down from the scaffolding.

"What's Baron doing up there?" Greg asked, following Joe's gaze.

"Let's find out," Joe replied in a growl.

Frank ran over to find out what was going on and managed to jump between his brother and Mike Baron before Joe could slam his fist into the reporter's face.

"It was an accident!" the reporter exclaimed. "I dropped my camera while I was climbing up the scaffold."

"What were you doing up there?" Joe snapped, straining against his brother's firm grip.

"I wanted to get a few dramatic shots," Baron replied in a tone that was somewhere between defensive and apologetic.

"Well, that last shot was pretty dramatic," Greg remarked dryly. "Too bad you didn't have another camera to take the picture."

Steve Swain stormed over and jabbed a finger at the reporter. "You're history, buddy. I didn't want you hanging around in the first place, and I draw the line when your careless actions put the team in danger. You're out of here."

"You—you can't do that!" Harold Jenkins spluttered. "He's writing an important article about Greg. He needs to be here!"

"Come on," Greg tried to cajole the instructor as Alice and Maria approached the group. "Cut the poor guy some slack. Nobody was hurt. He'll behave from now on." He turned to Baron. "Won't you?"

Anger flashed in the reporter's eyes, but then he sighed and nodded.

"I still don't like it," Swain grumbled. "He's your responsibility," he told Greg in a stern tone. "You brought him here. You keep him in line—and on a short leash."

"Yes, sir!" Greg responded, snapping to attention and saluting crisply.

"Save the theatrics for the movies," Swain snapped and walked back to the other campers.

"I think I'll go to my hotel to put my notes in order," Baron murmured stiffly.

Greg turned to the Hardys and smiled. "Alone at last. I thought they'd never leave."

"You may think this is all funny," Frank said, "but you could be in real danger. There have been three so-called accidents in three

57

days, and they all happened around you. Any one of them could have killed you. What do you know about this reporter?"

Greg rolled his eyes. "I'm going to get you guys some trench coats and fedoras. Give it a rest, will you? There's no secret conspiracy to kill me, okay?"

Frank didn't think it was okay, but he didn't press it with Greg. Something was seriously wrong at Space Academy, and Frank was determined to uncover the cause of all the mysterious accidents.

The next morning a small mob of reporters was waiting in front of Space Habitat when the Hardys came out with Greg and Harold.

Frank noticed that Harold didn't seem surprised to see the reporters. He also noticed that Harold grew more than a little perturbed when the focus of the media blitz shifted from Greg rescuing Joe on the Zero "G" Wall to Joe saving Greg's life in the shadow of the Saturn rocket.

"Weren't you concerned about your own safety when you rushed under the path of that falling camera?" a woman asked Joe, thrusting a microphone in his face.

"Well, I—I—" Joe stammered.

He dodged a microphone that poked at him from the side.

"Is it true that you shielded Greg Fontana with your body?" another reporter called out.

"That's not exactly—" Joe tried to respond.

Somebody else fired off another question that Joe didn't catch.

"All right! All right!" Harold Jenkins cut in, shoving the microphones out of Joe's face. "That's enough! We have a busy schedule today, and we have to get going."

Harold hustled Greg away from the throng of reporters. Joe ducked under a few more waving microphones and followed Greg.

Frank stood off to the side, watching the whole scene. On the edge of the crowd he spotted Mike Baron by himself with a slight smirk on his face. Frank didn't know if Baron had tipped off the media about Joe's heroic deed, but the reporter clearly enjoyed the fact that Joe's exploits had stolen the spotlight from Greg Fontana.

Four days into the program, Frank was into the rhythm of the Space Academy routine. A hard physical workout first followed by a harder mental workout took up the morning hours. The campers spent the afternoon in the Training Center, working with the simulators and other equipment designed to prepare astronauts for space missions.

"This is the Multi-Axis Trainer," Swain told

the team when they met in the Training Center after lunch.

Frank studied the device behind the instructor. Three thick steel bands—horizontal, vertical, and diagonal—encircled each other. Set one inside the other, they formed the rough outline of a sphere, like a giant gyroscope. A padded chair in the center of the hollow sphere was connected to the inner two circular steel ribbons by a series of metal struts.

"A lot of things can go wrong in space," Swain said. "A slight miscalculation on reentry could put the shuttle into an uncontrollable spin. When everything is tumbling in three directions at the same time, it's easy to get disoriented and confused. If that happens, you're dead.

"The Multi-Axis Trainer does exactly what you hope the shuttle never does. It spins you around in ways you didn't even know were possible."

"It sounds like one of those amusement park rides that make you dizzy and sick," Alice Culbert remarked.

"For the younger campers, that's about all it is," Swain replied. "For you guys we've added a little something extra.

"Come on up here," he said, gesturing to the short red-haired girl. "I'll show you how it works."

He led Alice to the chair in the middle of the device, helped her strap in, and then tapped a small panel next to the left arm rest. "See these colored squares on the panel? They'll blink on in a certain sequence. All you have to do is repeat the sequence by tapping the corresponding colored squares on the other panel on the right side. Got it?"

Alice nodded. "That sounds pretty easy."

The instructor smiled. "Yes, it does, doesn't it?"

He stepped out of the sphere and moved over to the control panel. "Oh, by the way," he added as he flipped a switch, "you have only a minute to get it right. Otherwise, you burn up when you hit the earth's atmosphere."

Sixty seconds later, Swain shut off the machine, and Alice wobbled out.

"You almost had it," Swain told her, holding her steady with one hand and guiding her off the platform. "Who's next?"

Greg, Harold, and Joe all took a spin in the whirling contraption with similar results.

Joe weaved an unsteady path back to where his brother was sitting on the floor and flopped down next to him. "Good luck," he said to Maria Galewski when she got up to take her turn.

"Luck has nothing to do with it," she responded as she walked up to the Multi-Axis Trainer.

Less than a minute after the device swung into motion, her ride was over.

"Forty-five seconds!" Swain announced as Maria stepped out of the chair with a smug grin on her face. "Congratulations. You're the first person this week to beat the machine."

Frank was the last victim. On his way up to the platform, he walked past Maria.

"I'll bet you five bucks you can't beat my time," she whispered.

Frank stared at her hard. She still had that self-assured smile on her face. "You're on," he said.

A few minutes later Frank forked over the money.

"I almost had it," Frank told his brother as they walked back to the dorm at the end of the session. "Just a few more seconds and I would have gotten the sequence right."

"A few more seconds would have been too late," Joe pointed out.

"And remember the words of our instructor and mentor," Greg added, putting his hands on his hips and puffing out his chest. " 'You can't be late in space!' "

"How do you do that?" Joe asked when he stopped laughing. "You sounded almost exactly like Swain."

Greg shrugged. "Just one of my many talents."

When they reached the Space Habitat, Frank stopped at a pay phone—labeled Level Two Communications—on the second floor. "We'll catch up with you later," he told Greg. "We have to call our folks."

Joe was surprised. "We do?"

"Yes," Frank said firmly. "We do."

"Oh," Joe said. He waited until they were alone and whispered, "Who are we really calling?"

Frank picked up the phone and punched in the number for long-distance directory assistance. "Could I have the number for *Profiles* magazine in New York City, please?"

Frank dialed the number, cajoled his way through a receptionist and a secretary, and finally got the person he wanted.

"This is, ah—Able Baker," Frank said in a deep voice, "the director of the Space and Rocket Center in Huntsville, Alabama. Do you have a reporter named Mike Baron on your staff?"

"Yes," the woman on the other end of the line said. "He's one of our best reporters. Why? Is there some kind of problem?"

"Nothing serious," Frank said. "But there have been a few—incidents."

There was a brief silence on the other end of the line. "Oh, dear," the woman finally responded. "I knew I shouldn't have let Mike cover the story on Greg Fontana. Mike has quite a temper, and I don't think he'll ever forgive Fontana for what happened."

"For what happened?" Frank shifted the phone to his other ear and held the receiver so Joe could listen to the conversation.

"Yes," the woman replied. "Greg was horrible to Mike's sister. I was afraid Mike might try to get revenge."

Chapter
7

"WHAT DO YOU MEAN, revenge?" Frank demanded as Joe bent closer to the telephone receiver, straining to hear every word.

"Mike assured me he didn't hold a grudge against Greg," the woman on the other end of the line said, defending herself. "It all happened a long time ago."

"*What* happened a long time ago?" Frank nearly shouted.

"Mike Baron's younger sister, Jessie, was on *Family Trouble* with Greg Fontana," the magazine editor replied. "She played Greg's sister on the series. Greg was the star of the show, but Mike's sister gained a following of her own after a while.

"As her popularity grew, Greg became more and more difficult on and off the set. Finally, he refused to work with her anymore. The producers decided that Greg was most important to the show, so Mike's sister was forced off the series.

"And that was the end of Jessie Baron's acting career," the editor concluded.

"That might explain a lot," Frank said. He talked to the woman for a few more minutes and assured her that she didn't have to take Baron off the story and send down another writer.

"I want Baron here where we can keep an eye on him," Frank told his brother after he hung up the phone. "We don't want him to disappear before we can crack this case."

The Hardys left the lobby of the dormitory and walked up to their room on the top floor, where they found Greg Fontana and Harold Jenkins. Greg was sitting on his bed, looking at a book.

"Hey, Greg," Frank said casually, tossing his workbook on the desk in the corner and sitting down on the edge of Joe's bed. "Joe and I were just talking about that television show you used to be on, and Joe remembered something kind of funny—didn't you, Joe?"

Joe blinked and stared at his brother. "I did?"

"Sure," Frank prompted. "It was about the girl who played Greg's sister." He turned to face the actor. "What was her name?"

Greg glared at Frank. "Something tells me you already know."

"Are you talking about Jessie Baron?" Harold spoke up. "Forget her. She's nobody."

"Not anymore," Joe remarked bluntly.

Frank kept his eyes on Greg. "Did you know Mike Baron was her brother?"

"So what?" Greg responded impatiently. "It's ancient history. And if you heard any of those rumors that I got her fired—that's all they are, rumors."

"Don't you understand?" Frank replied. "What really happened doesn't matter. All that matters is what Mike Baron *thinks* happened."

"And if he thinks you ruined his sister's career," Joe added, "he might be out to settle the score."

Greg threw his book down on the bed and stood up. "I've had enough of this," he snapped. "Get this through your thick skulls. Nobody's out to get me. This mysterious, invisible psycho killer you've dreamed up only exists in your heads."

The pay phone out in the hall rang a few times and then stopped. "Is there anybody around here named Hardy?" a voice called out.

Joe stuck his head out the door. "Who wants to know?"

The guy holding the receiver held it out toward Joe. "You've got a phone call."

Joe took the phone. He figured the call was from his father or mother. Even though Fenton and Laura Hardy gave their sons plenty of freedom, they didn't let the two brothers forget that they were still teenagers who eventually had to answer to their parents.

Joe was surprised when the voice on the phone said, "This is Mike Baron."

"What do you want?" Joe asked in a guarded tone.

"You probably saved my career," Baron said. "If Fontana had been hurt because of my clumsiness, I'd be finished as a journalist. A reporter with a reputation for killing celebrities would have a hard time finding work."

"Why are you telling me this?" Joe responded.

"I guess I'm trying to thank you," the reporter said. "But I'm not doing a very good job. Anyway, I'd like to buy dinner for you and your brother. It's the least I can do. There are a couple of pretty good restaurants in Huntsville."

Joe balked. He didn't trust Baron, but he didn't want to pass up the chance to question the reporter. He also hated to pass up a free meal. "I don't suppose they have a decent Chinese restaurant within a hundred miles of here," he said.

Baron chuckled. "That's what I said the first night I hit town. But I actually found a pretty good one. What time should I pick you guys up?"

"We'll meet you there," Joe responded. "We have a car we rented at the airport."

The reporter gave him the directions to the restaurant, and they agreed to meet there at seven that evening.

The spicy dinner was just what Joe needed after four days of cafeteria food. Halfway through the meal, Joe stopped picking at his sweet and sour shrimp with wooden chopsticks and attacked the plate with a fork. The Chinese might have honed their cooking skills during two thousand years of civilization, he told himself, but they still had a lot to learn about utensils.

The Hardy brothers were a great team. While Joe worked on the food, Frank worked on the suspect.

"You're staying at the hotel next to the Space and Rocket Center, right?" Frank asked casually.

Baron nodded. "I wanted to go through the Space Academy program with Fontana and get some real up-close material, but the administration wouldn't go for it. They thought an adult in the class would be disruptive."

"You're lucky you didn't have to be 'up close' to that fire in the dorm room," Frank said.

"Not really," the reporter responded. "That's the kind of material that makes for great magazine articles." He paused and smiled ruefully. "I was only a few hundred yards away. But I was sound asleep in my comfy hotel bed and didn't even hear the sirens. I must be losing my edge."

"And then you missed all the excitement on the Zero 'G' Wall, too," Frank said.

Baron's expression changed to a triumphant grin. "I didn't miss a second of that show. I was way in the back with the tourists, behind the railing that blocks off the training area. I even got a few good shots of the dramatic rescue." He looked at Joe. "Those were the last pictures I'll ever take with that camera."

Joe smiled. "You might still get some use out of it—as a paperweight."

Baron nodded, and Frank hit him with the next question. "Do you have a sister named Jessie?"

Baron stopped nodding and cleared his throat. "What do you know about Jessie?"

"We know she was on *Family Trouble* with

Greg Fontana," Frank replied. "And we know that she left the show under mysterious circumstances."

The reporter snorted. "There's nothing mysterious about it. Jessie's acting career was sacrificed on the altar of Greg Fontana's ego. That modest regular-guy routine is nothing but a front. It's all an act he puts on for the press."

"I take it that Greg is not one of your favorite people," Joe remarked.

"He's a two-bit Hollywood phony," Baron said. "If his comeback weren't news, I wouldn't give him a second thought."

"Then why were you so eager to cover the story?" Frank probed.

Baron leaned back in his chair, raised his eyebrows, and gazed evenly at Frank. "Why do I get the feeling I'm being interrogated?"

"Don't take it personally," Joe said. "Frank likes to ask questions. He's just naturally nosy."

"I'm a reporter," Baron responded flatly. "I've done my share of ambush interviews. So let's stop dancing around and get right to the point. I don't like Greg Fontana. I don't like a lot of the people I write about. I have a certain personal interest in this story, but I didn't come down here to get even—if that's what you think.

"If anything," he continued, "I should *thank*

71

Fontana for what he did to my sister. Instead of growing up to be a cardboard Hollywood cutout, Jessie got a chance to do something meaningful with her life. After she graduates from college in a few years, she's going to medical school."

Baron stood up and tossed some money on the table. "That should cover the bill. Suddenly I'm not very hungry. I guess I still get a little upset when I think about that whole ugly business."

Frank couldn't help wondering how often Baron thought about it and what those thoughts might drive him to do.

The Hardys got their first look inside the shuttle simulator the next day during their training session. The flight deck controls looked like the real thing to Frank. The command and pilot seats were surrounded by toggle switches, meters, and color-coded panels of glowing buttons. The forward control panel held three video monitors that could display information from the ship's computer systems or video images from cameras mounted outside the shuttle and in the cargo bay.

Frank took a deep breath and studied the imposing array of controls. He had only a couple of days to learn how to use them all. Swain had just announced the mission assignments, and Frank landed the pilot's spot. That meant he would have to help the mission commander "fly" the shuttle.

"Today we're going to practice a little EVA with the RMS," the instructor told the team, crowded around the flight deck.

"That sounds A-OK to me," Joe quipped. "But what does it M-E-A-N?"

Maria Galewski's glance was withering. "Extra Vehicular Activity using the Remote Manipulator System."

"I see our payload specialist has done her homework," Swain said. "So she'll take the first crack at the RMS controls." He turned to Frank. "Suit up. You get to be the first space walker."

Joe and Alice helped Frank into the bulky white spacesuit. Then he climbed through the airlock into the cargo bay.

"Okay, Frank," Swain's voice crackled in the tiny speaker in the spacesuit helmet. "Maria's going to lower the RMS. Be careful out there. The RMS is big and, and it's heavy—and it packs a nasty punch if you get in its way. So keep an eye on it and don't get too close to the unit until I tell you. Do you copy?"

Frank checked out the robotic arm bolted to the cargo bay wall. The arm was fully extended, reaching up through the open overhead cargo doors. Frank craned his neck and peered up through his tinted visor at the other end of the RMS, a good thirty feet above the shuttle. "Roger. I copy."

The arm jerked and swayed as it moved down slowly. Frank stepped back, giving the device a wide berth. Suddenly the RMS unit swerved sharply and whipped right at Frank. He tried to jump out of the way, but he was about as nimble as a stuffed rhinoceros in the clumsy spacesuit.

"Hey!" he yelled as he stumbled and fell backward. Unable to stop himself, he crashed onto the cargo bay floor, staring up helplessly as the gigantic robotic arm started down toward him with killing force.

Chapter

8

FRANK FRANTICALLY TWISTED and rolled in an attempt to dodge the mechanical monster. The mammoth arm smashed down on his leg. The thick, heavy spacesuit took the brunt of the blow, but a throbbing jolt of pain warned Frank that the suit wouldn't protect him next time.

The robotic arm jerked back up and wavered uncertainly in the air. Frank didn't wait for the fifty-foot-long device to strike again. He struggled to his feet, his eyes searching for an escape route. The overhead shuttle bay doors, stretching the whole length of the cargo bay, were wide open, but there was no way Frank could climb up the cargo bay wall in the ungainly spacesuit.

There was only one way out. Frank ducked another wild swipe from the RMS and lumbered toward the airlock. He felt as if he were caught in a dream, running through molasses in slow motion.

The robotic arm careened wildly around the cargo bay. Frank dove for the airlock. The heavy suit brought him down short of his goal. A shadow on the floor traced the deadly path of the RMS as it hovered over him. Frank rolled over and flattened himself against the curved wall of the cargo bay.

The jointed, metal arm flexed and started down again with a vicious hammerlike motion. There would be no escape this time.

In midswing, though, the robotic arm jerked to an abrupt stop, shuddered, and froze less than a foot from Frank's head. He waited for a few tense, breathless seconds. Then he edged his way over to the airlock, a wary eye trained on the giant metal arm.

Crawling through the low, narrow passage, Frank almost collided headfirst with Joe, who was rushing out to the cargo bay to help him. Joe backed out of the airlock, and Frank crawled back into the shuttle simulator.

"Are you okay?" Joe asked as he helped his brother out of the spacesuit.

Frank nodded. "I'll have an ugly bruise on my leg for a few days, but I'll live."

The rest of the team clambered down the ladder from the flight deck and crowded around Frank.

"It wasn't my fault!" Maria blurted out, an anguished expression on her face. "The RMS went crazy! If I tried to move it up, it went down. If I tried to make it go right, it went left. The thing had a mind of its own!"

"Something is definitely wrong with the RMS unit," Steve Swain confirmed. "When I saw what was going on, I grabbed the controls and almost knocked your head off myself. I finally just shut the unit down."

"I thought this was supposed to be *Space* Camp," Joe grumbled loudly, "not *survival* camp."

'You still don't get it, do you?" the instructor responded, turning his stern gaze on Joe. "Survival is the number-one mission objective. That's what I've been trying to teach you."

"There must be an easier way," Joe muttered.

"I know this team has had more than its share of bad luck," Swain said. "But just hang in there for a few more days. This is the kind of experience you'd never get in a classroom."

"What are we going to do about the remote manipulator system?" Frank asked.

"*We're* not going to do anything," Swain replied. "I'm going to pull the circuit board out of the RMS control panel and see if I can track down the malfunction."

The instructor dismissed the class, and the Hardys followed their teammates out of the shuttle simulator. As Frank walked across the main floor of the Training Center, he spotted Mike Baron on the high ledge at the top of the underwater training tank. A few feet away from the reporter, a couple of campers were adjusting their scuba gear for a dive into the tank. Frank didn't think that Baron even noticed them. Standing near the edge, with his hands on the safety railing, the reporter's eyes were focused on the team that had just come out of the shuttle simulator. And from his vantage point on top of the two-story cylinder, Baron had a clear view of the cargo bay from which Frank had barely escaped alive.

Frank and Joe didn't go back to the dorm with the rest of the team. Instead, they wandered off by themselves and found a deserted bench under a sprawling oak tree.

"This case is driving me crazy," Joe muttered.

Frank grinned. "That's a pretty short drive."

Joe glared at Frank. "I suppose you have it all figured out already."

"Not by a long shot," Frank said. "We have

at least two, and possibly three, suspects at this point."

Joe nodded. "Swain, Baron, and, after what happened today, we have to add Maria to the list. She was at the controls of the RMS when it went berserk.

"But why would she attack me?" Frank mused.

"Because Maria wants to be the best," Joe responded. "And the two best mission assignments are shuttle commander and pilot."

"So if she couldn't take the shuttle commander out of the picture"—Frank continued Joe's line of thinking—"she might try to eliminate the pilot."

"What's wrong with her being the payload specialist?" Joe said. "Swain said that was one of the most important jobs on any shuttle mission."

"The payload specialist doesn't get to *fly* the shuttle," Frank noted. "You don't even have to be an astronaut for that job—and Maria wants to be an astronaut."

"True," Joe said. "But how could she sabotage the controls for the robotic arm?"

"We don't know if there really was anything wrong with the controls," Frank replied. "Right now we only have Maria and Swain's word for it."

"But what if they were telling the truth?" Joe persisted.

Frank shrugged. "That wouldn't rule her out as a suspect. If any camper has the know-how to sabotage a piece of equipment like the RMS, I bet Maria does. I didn't see her in the cafeteria at lunch. She could have tampered with the unit then. Security around here is almost nonexistent."

"It's possible," Joe conceded. "Of course, we'd have to figure out how she figured out that you'd be the first guinea pig out the hatch."

"Good point," Frank said. "Maybe she didn't care who the victim was. Maybe she was so upset she just wanted to torpedo the whole program."

"Do you really think that's what happened?" Joe reacted.

"No, not really," Frank admitted. "We need to take a look at that circuit board from the control panel," he concluded. "If there's any evidence of sabotage, I'd be more likely to suspect Swain. All of these 'accidents' might be his idea of a good training program."

Joe stared at his brother. "Swain took the circuit board. He could destroy the evidence before anybody else sees it!"

*   *   *

The Hardys knew what they had to do. They went back to the Training Center and hung around until they saw Swain leave. Then they waited for most of the other team leaders and office workers to leave. When all was clear, they sneaked into Swain's office.

"Are you sure he left the circuit board in here?" Joe whispered.

"No," Frank admitted. "But I don't know where else to look if it isn't here."

Joe scanned the small, tidy office. "What does it look like?"

Frank shot a sidelong glance at his younger brother. "This is only a wild guess, but I'll bet it looks a lot like a circuit board."

"I know that," Joe responded, sounding a little miffed. "But how can we be sure we have the *right* circuit board?"

Frank sighed. "If you find more than one, we'll worry about it then. You check the file drawers in the desk. I'll see what's in the cabinets over on the wall."

The second cabinet yielded the prize. Frank pulled out the long, flat circuit board, ran his eyes over the miniature electronic city, and then turned the board over. He didn't have to be an techno-wizard to spot the problem. He expelled a low whistle as he traced the path of the hasty rewiring marked by a dozen sloppy soldering jobs.

"I think we hit pay dirt," he said.

"I think you're right," Joe responded. He pulled a soldering gun out of a desk drawer and held it up for his brother to see.

"I think you're in serious trouble," a deep voice intoned.

Chapter

9

FRANK FROZE at the sound of the intruder's voice. Joe whirled toward the door, still holding the soldering gun.

"Whoa, son," the man said. "You're not going to try to shoot me with that thing, are you?"

Joe glanced down at the electric tool. His fingers were wrapped tightly around the pistol-grip handle, the shiny metal heating element pointed at the man in the doorway. Joe realized that the thing looked a lot like a cheap toy ray gun from a science-fiction movie. He also pictured how stupid he appeared aiming the soldering gun at the guy who had just caught the Hardys ransacking Swain's office.

Frank stared at the man. He was wearing a blue uniform, but he wasn't a security guard or a police officer. "Colonel Housman?" Frank spoke up. "What are you doing here?"

"I was going to ask you the same question," the astronaut replied.

"Uh, this isn't what you think," Joe said lamely as he put the soldering gun down on the desk.

"What isn't?" Housman retorted sharply. "This is Steve Swain's office, isn't it? And you aren't Steve Swain, are you? And judging by the way you almost jumped out of your skin when I walked in, I'd say it's a fairly safe bet you aren't supposed to be here."

"I can explain," Frank said.

"I'm listening," Housman said flatly, his gaze shifting between the brothers. His eyes narrowed as he focused on Frank. "I remember you. You were at my lecture the other day. You claimed you had some unusual flying experience."

"It was more than a claim," Frank replied. "It was the truth."

The astronaut raised his eyebrows. "Well, I'm always willing to give a fellow pilot the benefit of the doubt." He glanced down at his watch. "You have exactly one minute to tell me why I shouldn't turn you over to security."

Frank talked fast. The single minute

stretched to five as Housman listened intently, and Frank described the events that had led the Hardys to Swain's office.

A frown creased the astronaut's face as he considered all of Frank's information. "I've known Steve Swain a long time, and he's a good man. A lot of the kids at Space Academy don't like him because he's a tough—but that's because Steve knows how tough it is even to be considered for NASA's astronaut training program."

"Getting cut from the shuttle program must have hit him pretty hard," Frank said.

Housman nodded. "I didn't realize how hard until now. If Steve Swain is responsible for all these incidents, he must have gone off the deep end. That's the only possible explanation."

"We can't prove anything yet," Frank pointed out.

Housman nodded at the circuit board in Frank's hands. "That may not be proof, but it's a fairly compelling piece of evidence. I still can't believe Steve would do something like this, but we can't take any chances. The safety of you campers comes first."

"So what do we do now?" Joe asked.

"I'll take you to see the camp director," Housman answered, "and you'll repeat everything you told me here."

"What do you think will happen to Swain?" Frank asked.

The astronaut sighed heavily. "This is a serious situation. The only sensible course of action for the director is to suspend Steve, pending a full investigation."

Colonel Housman was right, and the camp director didn't waste any time. Frank felt a little uneasy about the abrupt way the director handled the matter. Swain didn't get a chance to defend himself, and the Hardys didn't get a chance to talk to him before he left the Space and Rocket Center.

By dinnertime the word had gotten around.

"Have you heard the news?" Greg Fontana greeted the Hardys when they joined the actor and his assistant in the cafeteria.

"What news?" Joe asked.

"Swain is out," Harold Jenkins replied.

"Oh, that news," Joe said.

"It sounds like you know more about this than we do," Harold said.

"What do *you* know?" Frank responded.

Harold shrugged. "Not much. Some thick-necked bodybuilder type came by the dorm room and told us he was our new instructor. I asked him what happened to Swain, and he said Swain was on indefinite medical leave."

"Right," Joe muttered. "It's unhealthy for

him to be around us—but he's not the one who would have ended up in the hospital."

"All right," Greg said. "Let's have it. You guys obviously know the inside story. So give us all the juicy details or we'll be forced to start wild rumors about Swain being an outer-space alien spy."

"That may not sound so wild after you hear this," Frank said. "In fact, I'm starting to have a hard time believing it myself."

For the third time that day the Hardys explained why they went to Swain's office and what they found there. Frank did most of the talking, with Joe adding details here and there.

"I guess I owe you guys an apology," Greg said. "Somebody really *was* out to get me—and the rest of the team, too."

"Wait a minute," Harold said. "How does Mike Baron fit into this? He was the one who dropped the camera that would have reshaped Greg's head if Joe hadn't jumped in. You don't think Swain and Baron were working together, do you?"

Frank shook his head. "If Swain was responsible for the other incidents, then what happened at Rocket Park was just what Baron claimed it was—an accident."

Greg Fontana questioned Frank, *"If* Swain was responsible? Is there any doubt now?"

"I don't know," Frank answered. "I feel that

we put together a puzzle that has a few missing pieces. Instead of leaving holes for the missing parts, we forced the other pieces together. They don't fit together exactly, and the picture doesn't make sense."

Greg groaned. "Ever since that fire the first night here, you've been playing detective, searching for a secret plot and a nefarious villain. And you finally found one. Isn't that enough for you?"

"That fire is one of the things that bothers me," Frank said.

"I know I wasn't happy about it," Joe remarked. "My clothes still smell like smoke."

"That's not what I mean," Frank said. "I can understand why Swain might have tampered with the Zero 'G' Wall harness or the remote manipulator system to spice up the training program with a few real emergencies. But was there any real danger? Swain probably could have broken Joe's fall, and the one solid punch the RMS landed on me didn't do any serious damage.

"But if that fire in the dorm room had gotten out of control," he continued, "a whole lot of people could have been hurt or killed. Do you think Swain would do something like that?"

"I can't believe this," Greg said, a sharp edge to his voice. "Don't you know when to quit? You caught the bad guy. Congratulations. Good work. Now drop it, okay?"

Frank didn't respond. Joe glanced at his brother and knew the case was far from over.

After dinner they all headed back to the dorm. When they ran into Maria Galewski in the Space Habitat lobby, she pulled Frank aside.

"I'm sorry about what happened with the RMS," she said. "I honestly didn't mean to hit you with the robotic arm."

"It wasn't your fault," Frank assured her. "You didn't do anything wrong. Nobody could have controlled that thing."

"A good astronaut is prepared for emergencies," Maria countered. "I panicked."

Frank shrugged. "So consider the episode a valuable training lesson and learn from it."

Maria gave him a strange look. "Do you really think you'd make a better pilot than I would?" she asked him bluntly.

"I don't know," Frank answered. "I haven't given it much thought."

"Well, let's find out—right now," she said. "I beat you once on the Multi-Axis Trainer, and I can do it again."

"I'd like a chance to get my five bucks back," Frank said, "but the Training Center is closed for the night."

"I know a way to get past security," Maria responded. "Are you ready to go for it?"

Frank wasn't sure why he let Maria goad him into going along with her crazy dare. Maybe it was because it seemed so important to her, and he thought it might be a good way to find out more about her. Maybe it was because he needed to prove to himself that he could master the spinning, twisting contraption that had defeated him before.

Whatever the reason, Frank soon found himself strapped into the seat of the Multi-Axis Trainer. Maria stood at the controls, ready to start the computer-generated gyrations.

"Remember," Maria said, "you have to watch the way the lights blink on and off on the left-hand panel, then duplicate the sequence by pressing the same colors on the right-hand panel. When you get it right, the machine automatically shuts down."

Frank nodded. "I'm ready. Let's do it."

Maria hit the switch, and the Multi-Axis Trainer started twisting and turning. The colored lights near Frank's left hand started to blink just as the machine flipped him upside down and reversed the spin direction. Frank tried to focus on the lights, but every time he started to get the sequence, the diabolical device shifted and twirled him in a new direction.

Frank started to get dizzy, and he found it harder and harder to concentrate. His head felt as if it were spinning faster and faster. The fingers on his right hand fumbled over the touch panel, trying to match the pattern of lights flashing on and off on the left.

He knew he wasn't even close and was ready to accept defeat again. He just wanted his time to end so the world would stop whirling out of control.

"Okay!" he shouted when he was sure more than a minute had passed. "I've had enough! Turn it off!"

Maria didn't respond, and the Multi-Axis Trainer didn't slow.

"I give up!" Frank yelled. "You win!"

Maria still didn't answer. Frank couldn't keep his eyes focused, but he thought he could make out a blurred figure standing next to the controls.

"Shut it down!" Frank shouted. The machine responded by twisting and wrenching Frank around even faster and harder than before.

With growing horror, Frank realized that he had walked into a trap. Maria wasn't going to help him, and his ride was never going to end.

Chapter
10

THE MACHINE twisted and tilted, reversed direction, and jerked Frank along on the relentless course of a computer-simulated runaway spacecraft.

Frank didn't know how much more he could take. He was on the verge of passing out. He fought back the swirling blackness that threatened to engulf him and forced himself to concentrate on the panel of flashing lights. The lights blurred together and twirled around in a multicolored kaleidoscope.

He shook his head and narrowed his eyes. He blocked out all the whirling madness and locked his gaze on the panel, straining to bring the lights back into focus. The hazy, spinning wheel of shifting colors slowly resolved into separate blinking lights. But they seemed to be winking on and off in a random fashion.

Frank mustered every ounce of mental effort he had left and blocked out everything but the flashing lights. A repeating pattern finally emerged in lurching chaos. Slowly and carefully, Frank duplicated the sequence on the touch panel beneath his right hand.

An eternity after the ordeal began, the Multi-Axis Trainer responded to the coded sequence and shut down. As soon as the machine stopped moving, Frank bolted out of the seat and stormed over to the controls, where Maria Galewski stood with her arms folded in front of her, a faint smirk on her face.

"Nice job," Maria said. She glanced down at her watch. "It's a shame you couldn't have done it a little faster. You and the entire shuttle crew would be dead by now."

Frank glared at her. His head was still spinning, and he could feel a gigantic pain forming right behind his eyes. "Were you going to stand there and watch me spin around helplessly all night? Why didn't you turn the thing off when I told you to?"

"If you can't master the training equipment," Maria said, "you can't fly the shuttle. I knew you could do it if you thought your life depended on it."

"What if I couldn't?" Frank retorted.

Maria shrugged and walked away.

Dazed by his duel with the mechanical trainer, Frank stumbled back to the dormitory.

"What happened to you?" Joe was obviously startled when Frank staggered into their room. "You look like you were tumble-dried on the heavy-duty cycle."

Frank flopped down on his bunk with a soft groan. "I feel like that, too."

Joe didn't think his brother was hurt or injured, but he was a little worried by Frank's appearance. "Where did you go with Maria? I was going to follow you, but you waved me off when she dragged you out the door."

Frank looked at his brother. "When have you ever done what I told you to do?"

Joe shrugged. "There's always a first time. I figured you wanted a little privacy so you could soften up the ice queen." He grinned as he pictured the scene. "Then, when she was like putty in your hands, you'd slip in a few hard-hitting questions, and she would break down and confess."

Frank chuckled and glanced around the room. "Where are Greg and Harold?"

"They went over to the hotel to talk to Baron about the magazine article," Joe told him. "Now stop stalling and tell me what happened with Maria."

Joe shuddered when Frank told him about his encounter with the Multi-Axis Trainer. "You couldn't get me back in that whirling puke-mobile for a measly five-dollar bet. Maybe I'd do it for five *hundred,* but I'd have to give it some serious thought first."

"It wasn't one of my brighter moves," Frank admitted.

"Well, it wasn't a total loss," Joe said. "We found out that Maria isn't exactly squeamish about using rough tactics to get what she wants. That puts her near the top of my suspect list."

Frank nodded. "She wants to be in the driver's seat when our shuttle mission blasts off. At the very least, she was trying to rattle me so badly that I'd back down and let her take the pilot's job."

"I don't think she would have been too upset if that twirling torture chamber had taken you out of the picture completely," Joe said.

"The thought probably crossed her mind," Frank responded. "We'd better stay on our toes and keep our eyes open tomorrow. A careless move could be fatal."

"That sounds like something Swain would say," Joe remarked with a wry smile. "I wonder what the new instructor is like."

"We'll find out tomorrow," Frank replied.

* * *

The man with bulging muscles standing at the head of the classroom the next morning reminded Joe of the cartoon character made out of car tires that he'd seen in commercials. His almost perfectly round head was shaved. Joe didn't think the guy was much older than twenty-one or twenty-two.

"My name is Ron Thompson," the instructor told the class. "My job is to get you ready for your shuttle mission. I'm sure you've all learned a great deal here at Space Academy, but we still have a lot of ground to cover. Tomorrow, one team will get a chance to apply its new skills in the shuttle simulator. The other will work flight control.

"I know that sitting in a cramped, dimly lit room staring at computer monitors isn't glamorous," he continued, "but flight control is the heart of every shuttle mission. Without skilled experts handling operations on the ground, the shuttle would never reach orbit." He glanced down at a clipboard in his hand and then looked over the class. "Which one of you is Maria Galewski?"

Maria raised her hand.

"You'll be CAPCOM for tomorrow's flight," Thompson said. "Do you know what that means?"

"Yes, sir," Maria answered. "It means capsule commander."

"That's right," Thompson said. "Back in the days before the shuttle, astronauts were shot into space inside tiny, cramped capsules. The capsule commander was the leader of the mission team. We don't use capsules anymore, but we still call the flight commander CAPCOM."

"Hey, wait a minute," Harold Jenkins spoke up in an agitated voice. "Greg is supposed to be the shuttle commander."

"And he still will be—when the time comes," the instructor replied. "Tomorrow your team is working ground control. You'll be in the simulator the day after that." He checked his clipboard again. "Where is Janet Stephanopoulos?"

A gangly girl near the back of the room raised her hand.

"According to Swain's assignment list," Thompson said, "you're the shuttle commander for your team of six. Is that right?"

"That's right," the girl responded. "Where is Mr. Swain? When will he be back?"

The instructor shifted uneasily. "I'm afraid he won't be coming back—at least, not before you finish your course."

There were a few scattered murmurs among the campers.

"I know it's not fair to get stuck with a new instructor so close to the most important part of the program," Thompson said. "For what it's worth, Swain thinks you all have a lot of potential. He even warned me that a few of you know more about flying the shuttle than I do. And considering the fact that we have a couple of licensed pilots in the group, that wouldn't surprise me very much. The shuttle simulator is the only aircraft I ever piloted."

"You mean you don't have any *real* flying experience?" Maria asked sharply.

"Not too many of the instructors do," Thompson responded. "You were lucky to have Steve Swain showing you the ropes. That guy has experience with a capital *E.*"

For the next several hours, the class reviewed its responsibilities for the upcoming mission. Joe was relieved that they were finally doing something in the classroom that had a direct connection to what happened on the floor of the Training Center. All the lectures about plasma physics and astrobiology had been a little too much like, well . . . like rocket science.

Planning a mission was something Joe could appreciate. While the instructor explained the details of the various ground control duties, Joe's mind wandered a little, and he started to plan a mission of his own.

At lunch break Joe suggested that the six members of their team get together in the cafeteria to go over their assignments. Halfway through lunch, while Frank and Maria were deep into an intense debate about emergency abort procedures, Joe got up and announced that he had to get some notes from the dorm.

Frank was curious. The only "notes" Joe had from five days of lectures were random doodles scrawled in the margins of his workbook, which was tucked under his arm.

"Do you want me to come with you?" Frank ventured.

"I know you like to think I'd be lost without you," Joe quipped, "but I think I can find my way back to the dorm alone. Besides, it sounded like you and Maria were in the middle of something really important. You guys hammer out the details and let me know if there's anything I should know."

He made a hasty exit, hoping his brother got the hint. He needed Frank to keep Maria busy and away from the dorm.

Space Habitat was almost deserted. Joe had been counting on that. His plan hinged on getting in and out without being seen.

He climbed the stairs to the second floor. After a quick glance up and down the empty catwalk, he headed for the Space Academy girls' section. When he got to the room Maria shared with Alice Culbert and two other girls, he paused to check the catwalk again. Then he opened the door and slipped inside.

The lockers all had standard combination locks with a backup key slot. If a camper forgot the combination, a team leader could pop open the lock with a master key.

Joe didn't have a master key. He didn't need one. He took a thin metal lock pick out of his wallet and began working swiftly and silently. Because he didn't know which locker was Maria's, he started with the closest one. He had it open in less than a minute. It took even less time to find a purse with a Florida driver's license that identified the owner as Karen Shields.

Joe moved to the next locker. The lock sprang easily with just a few twists of the pick. He'd finish up quickly even if he had to go through all the lockers to find the right one.

Things were running smoother than Joe expected, when the metal pick suddenly snapped off in the third lock and he cut his finger on the jagged edge of the pick that was stuck in the key slot.

The situation took a serious nosedive when Joe glimpsed a massive shadow out of the corner of his eye, and a heavy fist clamped down on his shoulder. Behind him, a harsh voice said, "This is the end of the line for you, buster."

Chapter

11

THE HAND CLUTCHED Joe roughly and spun him around. A large woman in a blue team leader's flight suit glared down at him. Joe straightened up to his full height, but he still had to look up to meet her gaze.

Joe returned her angry scowl with a friendly smile. "Is there some kind of problem?"

"*You* are the problem," she snapped. "What are you doing in here?"

"What do you mean?" Joe asked innocently.

"You know what I mean," the counselor retorted. "Boys aren't allowed in here."

Joe glanced around the room. "You mean this isn't *my* room? Gee, it looks just like it. Well, that explains why I couldn't get the locker open. I must have tried my combination at least fifty times."

"Nice try," the counselor responded, grabbing Joe's arm and dragging him out into the hall. "If you can't come up with a better story, we'll see what the camp director thinks of that one."

"There you are!" a voice called out from down the hallway. Maria Galewski walked up to Joe with Frank right behind her.

"Do you know this boy?" the counselor asked sharply.

Maria looked at Joe. "I *told* you you'd get in trouble, didn't I?"

"That's right," Frank spoke up. "She did."

"You know how boys are," Maria said to the woman. "They rush off and do the *dumbest* things without thinking. I left some notes in my room, and Joe decided to get them for me."

Maria rolled her eyes and continued in a singsong whine. "I'm just a poor, pathetic *girl* and can't do anything for myself." She sighed wearily. "What makes boys think we'll be impressed if they treat us like babies?"

The counselor grunted and eyed Joe with disdain. "I'll let you off with a warning this time," she said sternly. "Don't let me catch you around here again."

"Have you ever considered a career in law enforcement?" Joe asked the woman. "You sound just like a police officer I know back home."

"Don't push your luck," the counselor growled. "Get out of here before I change my mind."

"He's gone," Frank said, grabbing Joe and hustling him down the corridor.

Maria caught up with them downstairs in the lobby. "You're not in the clear yet," she said, glowering at Joe. "I only got you out of that jam because we need you on the team. Frank thought you were gone too long and begged me to come rescue you. But I want to know what you were doing in my room, and I want to know *now*."

"Well," Joe began slowly, frantically groping for a good excuse, "it's a little hard to explain."

"Let me try," Maria said tersely. "You guys think something weird is going on around here, and you think I'm involved somehow."

Joe gave her a startled look. "How did you know that?"

"I have eyes, ears, and a brain," Maria replied. "First there are a bunch of bizarre accidents, and then suddenly we get a new instructor. So, obviously, somebody doesn't think the accidents were very accidental, and Swain is the number-one suspect."

She turned to Frank. "Am I right so far?"

"So far," Frank said.

Maria's sharp gaze shifted back to Joe. "But maybe somebody else doesn't think Swain did it. So they try to find somebody else to pin the blame on—like a pushy girl who isn't afraid to fight for what she wants."

"Let me apologize for my brother," Frank said. "He was way out of line. But you have to admit that—"

Maria whirled to face him. "Admit what?" she snapped. "When we found Joe upstairs with that team leader, you offered to trade mission assignments with me if I got him off the hook. Do you think I'd stoop to blackmail to get the pilot's job? I don't want anything I haven't earned."

Maria shoved Frank out of her way and stomped across the lobby. "It's getting late. We have a class in five minutes."

Frank patted his brother on the back. "Nice work, ace. I think we've made an enemy for life. What did you hope to accomplish with that stunt in Maria's room?"

"It seemed like a good idea at the time," Joe replied glumly. "That police detective who investigated the fire only searched the lockers in our section of the dorm. He never checked any of the girls' rooms."

"I see," Frank said. "So you thought you

might find incriminating evidence in Maria's locker."

"That was the general idea," Joe muttered.

"And a fairly pathetic one, too," Frank said. "She'd have to be incredibly stupid to hide evidence in her own locker, and Maria is definitely not stupid. It didn't take her long to figure out that you wanted me to distract her back in the cafeteria.

"Now that I think about it," Frank added, "she'd have to be denser than the core of a black hole not to see through that lame routine of yours. If you had found anything in Maria's locker that might connect her to the fire or any of the other incidents, I'd suspect that it was planted."

Frank's words flipped a switch in Joe's head. "Swain's too smart to do anything like that either. If he was the one who mixed up the wires on the circuit board, he wouldn't have left the evidence in his office.

"On the other hand, maybe he was going to rewire it back to normal to cover up the sabotage," he added, trying to poke holes in his own logic.

Frank shook his head slowly. "It would be much simpler just to get rid of the circuit board and wipe out any evidence that might lead back to him. And even if he planned to fix the wiring, he would have stashed the circuit board in a more secure hiding place."

"You're right," Joe realized. "And he wouldn't have left the soldering gun lying around in an unlocked desk drawer." He thought about it some more and started to chuckle.

Frank gave him a strange look. "What's so funny?"

"Can you imagine what would happen if we tried to explain this to anyone?" Joe replied. "Your honor," he spoke in a solemn voice, "we will prove that our client is innocent *because* the evidence was found in his possession."

"I see what you mean," Frank said. "If we want to clear Swain, we'll have to track down the real culprit."

The Hardys spent the rest of the afternoon learning about the complex array of instruments that the ground control team would use to guide the shuttle into orbit and direct its actions in flight.

When the class ended, Joe still had one nagging question. "After all the stuff that's handled by the computers and the ground control team, what's left for the shuttle crew to do?"

"As little as possible," Frank answered as they left the classroom. "Their main job is to complete mission objectives once the shuttle is in orbit. Until it's time to bring the shuttle back to earth, the pilot and commander's primary responsibility is to make sure nothing goes wrong—and then fix it if it does."

"So much for the romance of space flight," Joe muttered. "Do you think Swain knew he was training for a job as an outer space handyman?"

"Why don't we ask him?" Frank responded, nodding to the far side of the training area.

Joe looked over and saw Swain walking toward the exit, gripping a large box with both hands.

The Hardys intercepted him at the door.

"Can we give you a hand?" Frank offered, opening the door for Swain.

"No, thanks," Swain replied. "It's a lot lighter than it looks. I didn't really need a box this big, but it was the smallest one I could find."

"What's inside?" Joe asked as they walked across the parking lot.

"Not much," Swain said, a trace of bitterness in his voice. "Just a few personal things from my office." He set the box down on the hood of a sleek silver sports car, unlocked the door, and shoved the box into the passenger seat. "This box is all I have to show for a lifetime of work. Ever since I was sixteen, I poured all my energy into a single dream. I spent so much time trying to get into space that I never took much interest in life right here on earth.

"When I came here on leave from the shuttle program," he went on, "all I wanted to do was pass the dream along to some of you kids."

"You can still do that," Frank said. "If you didn't do anything wrong, a full investigation will clear you."

"There isn't going to be any investigation," Swain responded. "The camp administration doesn't want any embarrassing publicity. They want a quiet, tidy solution. So I'm out, and they put a lid on the whole thing."

"Then we'll just have to pry the lid off and make a big, noisy mess," Joe said. "We're good at that."

Swain shook his head. "There's nothing you can do. Perry Housman couldn't even get the director to change his mind. After Perry took a close look at that circuit board, he knew it wasn't my work."

"How did Colonel Housman know that?" Frank asked.

"I have a degree in electrical engineering," Swain explained. "And I got a lot of additional training in the shuttle program. I could have rewired the RMS to do card tricks, and only an expert with a schematic could have tracked down the changes. Those sloppy solder connections were the work of an amateur."

Frank and Joe had to put the case on hold while they prepared for the next day's mission. They were up and ready for the launch at six in the morning.

Maria sat between Frank and Joe in the small flight control room. On one of the wall-mounted video monitors, the shuttle crew smiled and waved as they strapped into their positions on the flight deck.

Joe stared glumly at the confusing display of data on his computer screen. He flipped open his thick mission manual and suddenly wished he had spent a little more time studying it.

"Um," he murmured, leaning over to Maria, "would you mind trading places with me? I want to sit next to my brother."

"I'm the CAPCOM," Maria said tersely. "This is where I'm supposed to sit."

"Does it really make any difference?" Joe asked.

"If it didn't matter," Maria hissed, "I wouldn't be anywhere near you two creeps. But Frank is the instrumentation and communications officer, and I need to be near the INCO."

"Okay," Joe responded. "Then switch places

with Frank. That way we'll *both* be next to him, and everybody will be happy."

Maria stood up stiffly. "All right. At least I won't have to sit next to *you*."

When everyone was settled in, Maria glanced down at her mission manual and briskly flipped a series of switches. "Commencing final instrument check," she spoke into her headset microphone.

"Roger," Frank responded, tapping on his computer keyboard and watching the readout on the screen. "All systems are—"

He caught a whiff of something burning. Glancing around the flight control room, Frank spotted a thin wisp of smoke drifting up from the back of Maria's terminal. He realized instantly that there was a severe electrical problem.

"Don't touch anything!" Frank shouted in alarm.

Maria's finger was already pressing a blinking button on the control panel. Frank didn't know what kind of electronic cataclysm Maria might have accidentally unleashed by pressing the flashing button on the console, and he didn't plan to wait around to find out.

Frank ripped off his headset, jumped out of his seat, and hurled himself on top of Maria. Her chair skittered away from the control panel and toppled over, sending them both crashing down.

Joe spun around in his seat and gaped at Frank and Maria struggling on the floor.

"Get down!" Frank cried out as a shower of sparks spewed out of the control panel. Then Maria's computer screen exploded with a thunderous *whoom*.

Chapter

12

JOE THREW HIMSELF to the ground a split second before flames erupted from the ragged hole in the computer monitor. Glittering shards of glass rained down on Joe as he scrambled for cover.

The smoke and flames triggered the fire alarms, and the ceiling sprinklers responded with a twirling spray of cold water.

"Get off me!" Maria yelled, shoving Frank out of the way. She staggered to her feet and stared at the blasted, scorched remains of the control panel, smoldering and hissing in the downpour.

"Everybody out!" the instructor roared from the back of the room. He rushed over to Joe, lifted him up off the floor with one massive hand, and led him out the door.

Frank picked himself up and glanced around. Everybody else was gone but Maria. She was standing, gazing at the smoking ruins in wide-eyed shock. Twisted, frayed wires sputtered fitfully with electric sparks. Frank touched Maria's arm lightly. "Come on," he urged gently. "We'd better get out of here."

Maria turned her head and blinked at him. "Oh—right," she murmured in a dazed tone, water streaming down her face. "Sure."

They were both drenched, and water was still drizzling out of the sprinklers as they trudged across the deserted control room. Greg Fontana ran back in, took Maria's arm, and guided her across the slippery wet floor.

Frank soon discovered that the scene on the main floor of the Training Center was more chaotic than in the ravaged control room. Even though the brief fire was already out, fire alarms were still sounding all over the vast building. Campers were running around frantically, and counselors were trying to herd them out the fire exits.

The Hardys were swept up and separated in the tide of fleeing campers. Frank wandered through the restless crowd outside the Training Center, searching for his brother.

"What are you talking about?" Frank heard

Joe complain loudly. "Greg had nothing to do with it!"

"Sure he did!" Harold Jenkins's petulant voice rose in response.

Frank pushed through to find Mike Baron trying to settle a dispute between Joe and Harold. Greg Fontana was standing off to the side, out of the fray.

Frank stepped in and pulled his brother away from the actor's assistant. "What's going on here?" Frank asked Joe.

"That little pip-squeak was trying to make it sound like Greg was the hero when everything went blooey in the control center," Joe grumbled.

"He did come back for Maria and me after everybody else hightailed it out of there," Frank pointed out.

"Big deal," Joe muttered, glaring at Harold.

Frank decided to change the subject. "How long has Baron been here?"

Joe shrugged. "We ran into him while we were getting shuffled out of the building."

"He was *inside?*" Frank asked.

Mike Baron walked over before Joe could answer. "Hey, Frank, Greg was telling me about how you helped him rescue the team from the electric fire in the control room."

"What?" Joe burst out. *"Greg* said that?" His face became an angry red. He shouldered past the reporter and confronted Greg. "I've put up with your loud-mouthed little shadow until now because you seemed like a decent guy. If there was any hero in that disaster, it was Frank. What did you do that was so special? You ran out with everybody else and then ran back in after it was safe."

"Take it easy," Greg said, putting a hand on Joe's shoulder. "I know you're upset because you left your brother in the control room and didn't go back to save him yourself. But you were in shock, and everybody was running around and shouting in a confused panic. You didn't know what was going on. You shouldn't feel guilty about that."

Joe batted Greg's hand away and stormed off.

Frank ran after him and caught up with Joe in Shuttle Park. Riding on top of the huge external tank in the middle of the round plaza and angled toward the sky, the *Pathfinder* shuttle cast a long, early-morning shadow over the Hardys as they walked together.

"You have to give Greg credit for one thing," Frank said. "He sure knows how to act. That was quite a touching performance he gave back there."

"Maybe he was right," Joe said in a dejected tone. "Maybe I do feel guilty."

"There are at least three good reasons why

you shouldn't feel that way," Frank responded. "First, you didn't have any choice about leaving the control room. You were hauled out of there. Second, I came out about thirty seconds after you did. There wasn't time for you to do anything. And third, we don't have time for you to feel sorry for yourself. We have a case to solve."

"Don't remind me," Joe said glumly. "We aren't any closer to cracking this one than we were when we started."

"That's not true," Frank replied. "We've narrowed down our list of suspects."

"We can't rule out Swain yet," Joe remarked. "We don't have any proof that the evidence was planted in his office. Maybe he was just careless."

"Good point," Frank conceded. "But today's events blew a big hole in our theory about one of the other suspects."

Joe asked his brother, "What do you mean?"

Frank answered with another question. "Who was sitting at the terminal that exploded?"

"You were," Joe said. "No, wait—Maria was. You guys switched places."

Frank nodded. "That's right. Now answer this one: Do you think Maria would use a terminal that she knew was rigged to electrocute her or blow up in her face?"

"We don't know the terminal was rigged," Joe argued weakly.

Frank sighed. "Right. It simply decided to self-destruct. Accidents follow our team everywhere—but it's all merely an amazing series of coincidences. Is that what you think?"

"No," Joe admitted. "But Maria was starting to look like a prime suspect. And if we cross her off the list, who's left?"

"Do you remember what Baron said that made you fly off the handle and go after Greg?" Frank responded.

"Don't remind me about that either," Joe grumbled.

Frank smiled. "It was really very interesting. He said that Greg was telling him about how I helped him rescue the team from the *electrical* fire." He turned to his brother. "Who told him it was an electrical fire?"

Joe could see where Frank was leading. "The person who short-circuited the control panel wouldn't need to be told—whoever it was would already know."

"You read my mind," Frank said. "Every time something goes wrong, Baron isn't far away, but he's never close enough to the action to attract attention. I'm starting to think that's more than a little strange."

"This whole case is strange," Joe remarked.

* * *

The Hardys and the rest of the campers spent the rest of the day in the dormitory waiting to find out if they'd be able to use the Training Center again. Late in the afternoon the word came down that the center would reopen the next day. Ron Thompson stopped by the Hardys' dorm room and told them their mission would start in the morning as scheduled.

"That doesn't give us much time to prepare," Frank said after the instructor left.

"It also doesn't leave us much time to find out what's going on around here," Joe added.

"Not that again," Greg Fontana groaned.

Joe was about to reply but bit his lip and fumed silently. Relations in the room had been severely strained all day.

"I'm sick of studying," Greg complained. "And I'm sick of your detective stories. I'm going out to get some air." He jerked open the door and slammed it shut behind him.

Joe looked over at Harold Jenkins. "Aren't you going with him?"

"I'm not with Greg all the time," Harold replied in a huffy tone. "I have a life of my own, you know."

Joe was sorely tempted to suggest that Harold find someplace else to live it, but he held his tongue. He tried to concentrate on the material in his mission manual, and he managed to stick with it for almost an hour before he started getting cabin fever.

"Let's get out of here," he said to his brother.

"Okay," Frank responded. "Where do you want to go?"

Joe shrugged impatiently. "I don't know. Out. It doesn't matter."

The pay phone in the hall rang, and somebody called out, "Joe Hardy! You've got a phone call!"

Joe and Frank went out to the pay phone, and Joe picked up the receiver that had been left dangling by whoever answered the phone.

Joe instantly recognized the voice on the other end of the line. He covered the speaker with his hand and whispered, "It's Mike Baron! What should I do?"

"Find out what he wants," Frank suggested simply.

"Oh, right," Joe said. "What's up?" he said into the phone, trying to sound casual.

"We need to talk," the reporter said in an urgent tone.

"Okay," Joe replied. "Let's talk."

"Not on the phone," Baron said. "Can you meet me at the restaurant where we had dinner?"

"I guess so," Joe said hesitantly.

"Good," the reporter said. "Meet me there in fifteen minutes."

"That's cutting it a little close," Joe said.

"This can't wait!" Baron snapped. "You have to come now or it'll be too late!"

"Okay, okay," Joe assured him. "We're on our way."

Joe hung up the phone and grabbed the car keys out of the dorm room.

"Do you think Baron knows we suspect him?" Joe mused as they hustled across the parking lot to their rented car.

"It's possible," Frank said. "But even if he does, he's not going to do anything to us in a crowded restaurant. We might as well find out what he has to say."

He stopped at their rented car and waited while Joe opened the driver's door, got inside, and unlocked the door on the other side. As Frank slid into the passenger's seat, he caught a whiff of a naggingly familiar odor.

Joe noticed it, too. "What's that smell?" he asked, wrinkling his nose.

Frank twisted his head around and saw something very weird on the floor behind the driver's seat. There were two plastic containers, one taped on top of the other. The top one looked oddly misshapen, as if it had been half-melted by something. The noxious odor was definitely wafting up from the plastic contraption.

Frank suddenly remembered what the vaguely familiar smell was—and what would happen when the chemical in the top container burned through the plastic and reached the substance in the bottom container.

"Rocket fuel!" he cried out. "It's going to explode!"

Chapter

13

"GET OUT!" Frank yelled, shoving the car door open with one hand and grabbing Joe's arm with the other.

Joe barely got out a startled "Hey!" before Frank bolted out of the car and jerked him across the seat.

"Come on!" Frank shouted desperately, tugging on Joe's sleeve. "It's going to blow!" The fabric ripped, and Frank tumbled backward, clutching a torn scrap of Joe's shirt.

Joe had no idea what Frank was talking about, but he didn't think this was a good time to stop to ask questions. Frank wanted him to go out the passenger door, so out he went.

The driver's seat erupted in a ball of orange

flame. The blinding flash seared Frank's eyes, and a piercing *ka-boom* roared in his ears. In the painful, dazzling glare of the fireball that engulfed the car, Frank made out the dim outline of a figure hurtling through the air, caught in the shock wave of the blast. "Joe!" he cried in horror as the figure crashed onto the ground.

Frank tried to stand. Another blast ripped the air as the gas tank of a nearby car exploded from the intense heat. Frank stayed down low and crawled over to where his brother's body lay sprawled on the pavement, deathly still.

"Joe!" he shouted. "Joe!" Frank couldn't hear his own distraught cries. The deafening blast was still ringing in his ears.

Joe couldn't hear him either. He was far away. First, he was flying. He liked that part. He was as free as a bird, soaring above the clouds.

Then he was falling, tumbling and plummeting out of the sky. He wasn't too wild about that part.

Then the ground delivered a painful lesson on the laws of gravity, slamming into him with a stunning blow. He definitely didn't care for that part.

Joe groaned. His whole body ached. He opened his eyes and stared up into his brother's alarmed face.

"You're alive!" Frank exclaimed.

Joe winced. "Could you turn down the volume a little? You're loud enough to wake the dead."

Frank laughed as a flood of relief washed over him. "You don't know how close that is to the truth. I thought you had checked out for good. That blast packed enough punch to kill a bull elephant."

"I'll remember to use a car bomb the next time I run up against a bull elephant," Joe replied. He sat up and looked over at the blazing wreck that would have been their coffin if Frank hadn't reacted with lightning-fast reflexes. "I bet we won't get our deposit back now," he said.

Campers and counselors poured out of the dormitory to see the inferno that now engulfed three cars in the parking lot. The fiery heap of twisted steel marked the source of the thunderous blast that had ripped through the night, rattling the windows and echoing down the corridors.

Fire trucks and police cars with wailing sirens arrived on the scene. Police officers pushed the curious onlookers back a safe distance while firefighters doused the flaming wrecks. Joe was still a little dazed when Detective Walsh collared him and shoved him into an unmarked car with Frank.

"This has gone far enough," Walsh said gruffly.

Joe touched a raw scrape on his forehead where the pavement had reminded him that flying without wings could end with brutal results. "Tell me something I don't already know."

"I was hoping you'd tell *me* something along those lines," Walsh said.

"I have this weird feeling that we've had this conversation before," Joe replied.

"And we'll keep having it until I find out what's going on here," Walsh snapped.

"When we find out," Frank interjected in a firm, calm voice, "you'll be the first to know."

Walsh's steely gaze shifted to Frank. "I think you already know. I think you were playing around with something that blew up in your faces."

"That's one way to look at it," Frank said, "and it might not be too far from the truth. But if you think we had anything to do with the explosion that totaled our car, you'll have a very hard time finding any proof."

The detective glanced out the window at the smoldering remains of the rental car. "You boys aren't dealing with a bunch of idiots. We can bring in forensic gear that'll make you think you're in a science-fiction movie. We'll find out what caused that blast."

"And I'll tell you what your forensic experts will find," Frank responded. "They'll find traces of nitrogen tetroxide and monomethyl hydrazine. Mix those together and you get a nice big bang."

"What were you planning to do with that explosive mixture?" Walsh asked sharply.

"We planned to get as far away from it as fast as we could," Joe answered. "Unfortunately, we couldn't get far enough fast enough."

Walsh frowned. "Why did you want to blow up your own car?"

Frank sighed. "We didn't want to blow up anything. We didn't know the stuff was in the car until it was almost too late. Somebody planted a homemade bomb in the backseat."

"What triggered the bomb?" Walsh probed. "If it was wired to go off when you got in the car or started the engine, you wouldn't be sitting here now. You'd be strewn all over the parking lot."

"It wasn't wired to anything," Frank replied. "The bomb had a very crude but effective time delay. Hydrogen tetroxide becomes highly corrosive when it's exposed to moisture. So put a little water in it, and you've got a great acid that eats a hole in the bottom of the container and keeps going until it hits the monomethyl hydrazine."

"That still doesn't explain what set off the bomb," the detective argued. "Something would have to ignite the mixture."

"The two compounds ignite on contact," Joe explained. "It's called a hypergolic reaction."

The detective narrowed his eyes. "If you didn't make the bomb, how do you know so much about it?"

"The mixture is used as fuel for the shuttle's on-board maneuvering system," Frank said. "Our instructor gave us a great pyrotechnic demonstration the very first day of class."

"You'd be amazed at what you can learn around here," Joe remarked.

"Hold on," Walsh said. "Are you telling me that there's a supply of these chemicals right here at the Space and Rocket Center?"

Frank nodded.

"And everybody at Space Academy knows that you can make an explosive device by mixing the stuff together?"

Frank nodded again. "And almost anybody could have stolen the materials to make the bomb. Security isn't very tight."

The detective groaned. "That means I've got over two hundred suspects!"

"Give us a little time," Frank said, "and we might be able to narrow down the search for you."

The detective squinted at him. "If you know anything, you'd better tell me now."

"If we knew anything you could use to make an arrest, we would tell you," Frank said.

"I don't like this," Walsh grumbled. "I'm going to let you go—but don't leave town."

Joe looked out the window at the charred steel skeleton, steaming and hissing in a shallow pool of black water. "Don't worry. We won't be going anywhere for a while."

Frank and Joe got out of the police car and were instantly mobbed. Joe ignored them. His attention was riveted on a figure that was hovering around the wreckage. He bolted past the crowd, jumped over the yellow police tape that blocked off the blasted remains of the cars, and charged toward the man.

"Baron!" he roared, grabbing the reporter and twisting the man around to face him. "You set us up! We can't prove it yet, but we will. We'll nail you for this. I guarantee it."

"What?" the startled reporter reacted. "Was this *your* car?"

"You know it was," Joe growled. "And you made sure we'd be in it when the bomb went off."

"I don't know what you're talking about," Baron responded, pulling away from Joe.

"Let me refresh your memory," Frank said, coming up behind his brother. "You called us a few minutes before the blast and said you had to see us right away. You told us to meet you at the Chinese restaurant in town. You knew we'd have to drive there, and you were the *only* one who knew we'd go anywhere near the car tonight."

The reporter stared at Frank. "I didn't call you. If you don't believe me, you can check the hotel's records. They log all the outgoing calls."

"You didn't have to call from your hotel room," Joe countered. "You could have used a pay phone."

"But I *was* in my room," Baron replied. "And I *was* on the phone, but I didn't call you. I called my editor in New York. We had been talking for at least a half hour when the bomb went off.

"As a matter of fact," the reporter continued, "I should get back to the hotel and call her again. I hung up on her in the middle of a very interesting story when the explosion rocked the building."

Frank raised his eyebrows. "More interesting than attempted murder and exploding cars?"

Baron chuckled. "Not quite—even though it might mean I've wasted my time on this article about Fontana."

"Did the magazine cancel the story about Greg's comeback?" Frank asked.

"There may not be any comeback to write a story about," Baron answered. "The latest news from Hollywood is that Scott Randolph suddenly became available and is very interested in the part Fontana is supposed to play."

"Scott Randolph," Joe echoed. "I've seen a couple of his movies."

"He's a big star right now," Baron said, "and that means big business at the box office. If the studio can get Randolph, they'll dump Fontana."

Frank looked at the reporter. "Does Greg know about this?"

"He probably heard about it before I did," Baron responded. "His agent is a guy named Jonathan Healy, and Healy is hard-wired into the Hollywood gossip machine. Fontana may have even heard rumblings before he left Tinsel Town on his trip to Space Academy."

Most of the fire engines and police cars were gone by the time Frank and Joe headed back to the dormitory.

"I don't believe Baron," Joe muttered as they walked across the quiet lobby. "I'm sure that was his voice on the phone."

"I was just thinking about that," Frank said. "Remember the way Greg imitated Maria?"

"Sure," Joe responded. "It was pretty good, and his impression of Swain was right on the money. The guy has a lot of talent."

"That's what I thought, too," Frank said. "If I wasn't looking at him at the time, I would have thought it really was Swain talking."

"Me, too," Joe agreed.

"Greg could have pulled a great practical joke on us," Frank remarked casually, "if he had done his Swain voice over the phone."

Joe stopped and stared at his brother. "If Greg could fool us with his impression of Swain or Maria . . ." His voice trailed off as the realization crept up on him.

Frank nodded. "He probably could have conned us with a convincing imitation of almost anybody, including Mike Baron."

Chapter
14

"WHY WOULD GREG want to kill us?" Joe asked his brother.

"I don't think he was trying to kill us," Frank answered. "I think he just wanted to scare us off the case. The bomb was a pretty crude device. Maybe it was supposed to blow up before we reached the car, or maybe Greg didn't realize how powerful the blast would be."

"But why would Greg want us off the case?" Joe responded. "It doesn't make any sense."

"He was never exactly thrilled that we thought there was any kind of case to investigate," Frank reminded his brother. "And everything fits together when you consider what Baron told us.

"If Greg knew all along that his big movie comeback was in danger," Frank continued, "then that gives him a motive for staging those accidents."

Joe frowned. "It does? What was his motive?"

"Think about it," Frank said. "What happened after he put out the fire in the dorm room and after he rescued you on the Zero 'G' Wall?"

"A police detective grilled us and Steve Swain yelled at us," Joe responded.

"What happened the next morning, both times?" Frank prodded.

Joe retraced the events in his head. "We worked out until we almost dropped dead, then we worked on physics problems until my brain almost exploded."

Frank rolled his eyes and sighed. "What happened *before* all that—as soon as we walked out of the dormitory?"

Joe finally understood where Frank was leading. "We ran into a wall of reporters who were hanging on every word out of Greg's mouth." He paused a minute. "You couldn't ask for better publicity, could you?"

"It makes a certain kind of warped sense," Frank said. "With all the news coverage making Greg a big hero, the movie studio might think twice about dumping him for another actor."

Joe shook his head doubtfully. "I don't know. That sounds more like the kind of stunt Harold Jenkins would pull. He acted like he was running those news conferences. I think he called all the newspapers and television stations to make sure their reporters would show up."

"He probably did," Frank agreed. "And Greg knew that he would because that's part of Harold's job. Harold is Greg's biggest fan and his number-one promoter. But we know Harold didn't plant the bomb or make the call that lured us out to the car. He was in the dorm room with us."

"He could have put the bomb in the car earlier in the day," Joe argued.

"Not *that* bomb," Frank replied. "As soon as that thing was slapped together, the nitrogen tetroxide started to dissolve the container. I'd guess it didn't take more than fifteen minutes for that contraption to blow itself up."

"So Greg must have made the bomb and planted it himself," Joe conceded. "Do you think he was acting alone the whole time?"

Frank shrugged. "We may never know. We don't even have one solid shred of evidence linking Greg to any of the incidents."

"Then we'll just have to keep digging until

we find something," Joe said resolutely. "We can't let him walk away from this."

"I don't think he's ready to walk away yet," Frank told him. "Greg's an actor, a showman, and every performer knows you always save your best material for last. The show's a flop if you don't have a boffo climax."

"I see," Joe said. "Now would you mind translating that into English?"

Frank smiled. "What's the big climax of the Space Academy program?"

"The simulated shuttle mission," Joe answered. "All our training's been for it."

"That's right," Frank said. "I'll bet Harold has already made sure plenty of reporters will be on hand to witness Greg's performance as shuttle commander."

Joe raised his eyebrows. "And I'll bet Greg has quite a show planned."

"I think we'd better find out before we get in that simulator tomorrow morning," Frank replied.

Frank and Joe didn't have any trouble slipping past the security guard at the Training Center entrance, and they were soon padding across the dimly lit main floor to the shuttle simulator.

"What are we looking for?" Joe asked in a low voice as they climbed onto the flight deck.

"I don't know," Frank answered. "We'll have to comb the whole simulator and hope to find something."

"I'll start with the robotic arm controls," Joe said.

"Greg already sabotaged the remote manipulator system once," Frank reminded him. "He wouldn't do it again."

"He might," Joe contended. "If he thought it was the last place anybody would look, then it would be the best place to set his booby trap."

"That's an interesting theory," Frank remarked. "There's only one minor problem with it. Greg didn't know anybody was going to search the simulator for signs of sabotage before the mission."

"And if he did," Frank added, "he would make the tampering very hard to find."

"I'm going to check out the RMS anyway," Joe replied doggedly. "Part of our mission is to repair a satellite in orbit, and we're supposed to use the robotic arm for that. Greg could make himself look real good if he saved us all from a berserk giant metal arm."

Frank glanced at his younger brother. He knew there were times when it was useless to argue with him. "Okay," he said. "I'm going to take a look at the main control panel."

Joe switched on the RMS and watched the robotic arm on the video monitor while he worked the controls. "Everything seems okay here," he reported. "Hey, Frank," he added as he moved the arm up and down and back and forth a few more times to make sure. "Did you know you could move this thing outside the cargo bay?"

"Of course," Frank replied. "How would you use the RMS to repair an orbiting satellite if it couldn't reach outside the cargo bay?"

"That's not what I meant." Joe fiddled with the controls some more and switched the view on the video monitor to one of the outside cameras. "I mean I could reach out and scoop something up off the Training Center floor."

"That's great," Frank mumbled as he removed an access panel and stuck his head under the main flight controls. "But we didn't come here to play with the equipment. Keep looking around."

"I'm looking," Joe said. "I'm looking." He scanned the dials and switches that bristled all over the flight deck. "This is hopeless," he groaned. "We've got a couple thousand gizmos here. We can't test them all."

Frank crawled out from under the control panel. "You're right," he admitted reluctantly. "There are enough wires under there to reroute the entire New York phone system. Greg could have crossed a few hundred of them, and I might never spot a single one."

Frank got up off the floor and sat in the commander's seat. "We have to approach this methodically. Greg is the shuttle commander. What can the commander do that nobody else can do?"

Joe shrugged. "Beats me. I thought the ground control team and the computers could do just about anything except put salt on the space food sticks."

"That's it!" Frank reacted, jumping out the chair and heading for the exit.

"What's it?" Joe whispered loudly, chasing after his brother as he hustled across the training room floor. "Do you think Greg poisoned the food supply?"

"What would you do if you were an actor who found a terrific screenplay with a lousy ending?" Frank responded, heading into the mission control room.

"I hate it when you answer my questions with another question," Joe muttered.

Frank went past the flight control consoles and sat down at the instructor's computer terminal in the corner. "You'd write a better ending for the story," Frank told his brother.

"The simulated shuttle mission is like a movie screenplay," Frank explained as he tapped on the keyboard. "The simulator is run by computers, and the mission is the 'story' the instructors program into the computer."

Joe stared at the menus and windows of information flashing by on the screen. "What does this have to do with Greg's plan to sabotage the mission?"

"Greg doesn't want to ruin the mission," Frank said. "He wants something to go wrong that only he can fix. Then he can jump in and play the hero."

"I know that," Joe said. "But I still don't see the connection."

"The whole mission is right here in the computer," Frank said. "Everything that happens on the simulated mission is in the program, including any 'emergencies' that the crew run up against during the flight."

He turned back to the computer and started typing again, going through the menus and searching the files.

Now Joe understood what Frank was looking for. "Of course! The simplest way to create an emergency that only the commander can handle is to program it into the simulation!"

"And here it is," Frank announced, pointing at the computer screen. "Somebody has inserted a massive malfunction that will lock out all the controls on the ground and in the shuttle—except the shuttle commander's—right at the critical point when the shuttle reenters the atmosphere. Greg will get to land the shuttle by himself."

"And take all the credit," Joe added.

"Now let's see what we can do to throw Greg a few unexpected curves," Frank said. He started typing again, stopped, and slapped his forehead. "I forgot to put the access cover back on the control panel in the simulator."

"I'll take care of it," Joe responded. "You keep hacking," he added as he slipped out of the control room.

Frank turned back to the computer, and his hands moved across the keyboard. The program interface was easy to use, and it only took him a few minutes to make the changes he wanted. "That should do the trick," he murmured, smiling and leaning back in the chair.

"Very good," a cold, harsh voice spoke up behind him. "I didn't think you'd figure it out. Now I have to figure out what to do with you."

Frank spun around. A figure emerged from the shadows near the open door. It was Greg Fontana—and he was holding a gun.

Chapter

15

FRANK STARED at the pistol in Greg's hand. "Greg," he said, forcing himself to sound calm, "what are you doing?"

"What does it look like?" Greg snapped. "I'm pointing this gun at you."

"I can see that," Frank said. "But what are you going to *do* with it? Shoot me? Even if you hide my body, what do you think will happen to the shuttle mission if the pilot is missing at launch time?"

"Shut up!" Greg growled, waving the pistol at Frank. "I'm trying to think."

"Take your time," Frank said in a subdued tone. "Don't make any hasty decisions—like you did with that car bomb."

"It's your own fault," Greg berated Frank. "Everything was going perfectly until you started snooping around. The plan was so simple. A few harmless accidents, and nobody gets hurt. What's the harm in that?"

There was a tense edge in Greg's rising voice. "But you just couldn't leave it alone, could you? You and your brother have been the most incredible pains! Who do you think you are? Sherlock Holmes and Dr. Watson? You're nothing! I'm Greg Fontana!

"And I still have a chance to be somebody again. I won't let you ruin it."

"You'll ruin any chance you might have if you use that gun," Frank responded. "Nobody's been hurt yet. Put the gun down, and we can work this out."

Greg let out a short, bitter laugh. "You still sound like a bad movie." He motioned at the door with the pistol. "Let's go. And put your hands up," he added with a nervous jerk of the gun.

"Anything you say," Frank said. "But be careful with that thing.

"Where are we going?" Frank asked as they moved across the training room floor.

"Keep your mouth shut," Greg growled, jabbing Frank in the back with the pistol. "Just do what I tell you."

"You're in charge," Frank assured him.

"What did I just tell you?" Greg snapped. "Shut up!"

Frank heard a low mechanical hum coming from the direction of the shuttle simulator. The sound didn't mean anything to him at first, but when a few whirs and clicks were added to the mix, the faint noise stirred up a very vivid memory. Frank kept his eyes straight ahead, not daring to even glance over toward the simulator. He didn't want to do anything that might tip off Greg.

"Hold it!" Greg ordered sharply. "What's that noise?"

"Noise?" Frank said. "What noise? I don't hear anything."

"Shut up!" Greg hissed. "I'm trying to—"

"Oof!" The startled grunt whistled out of Greg's mouth as a vicious blow slammed into his side. He whirled around to face his attacker.

Frank bolted for cover.

"Stop or I'll shoot!" Greg shouted.

Frank didn't know if Greg was yelling at him or his assailant. He decided it didn't matter. He kept running and dove behind the Multi-Axis Trainer.

A sharp *crack* followed a split second later by a metallic *spang* told Frank that Greg knew how to use the gun. He had hit his target.

Frank peered out to see if the pistol was any match for the remote manipulator system.

"Keep away from me!' Greg screamed, staggering backward as the huge robotic arm took another swipe at him. He fired twice wildly, missing the swooping metal device both times. He stumbled and fell. The gun flew out of his hand and skittered across the floor.

Frank jumped up and sprinted after the gun.

Greg scrambled to his feet, dashed across the floor, and scooped up the weapon before Frank had covered half the distance. "Don't come any closer!" Greg yelled, whipping the gun around to point it at Frank.

Frank gritted his teeth and put on an extra burst of speed.

"I'm warning you!" Greg cried out.

Frank was close enough now to see Greg's finger on the trigger. One little squeeze and Frank would be history. But he was long past the point of no return.

Frank ducked in under Greg's outstretched gun arm and grabbed Greg's wrist with his left hand. Then, in one swift blur of motion, he pivoted around, swung his right arm up under Greg's armpit, and clamped his right hand on Greg's arm, close to his shoulder.

The rest was all leverage. Frank flipped Greg over his shoulder with a classic judo throw. Greg crashed down on his back, with Frank standing over him, still gripping his wrist. With his foot in the actor's armpit and both hands firmly grasping the wrist holding the gun, Frank jerked Greg's arm upward with a quick, sharp tug.

Greg cried out in pain. His fingers went limp around the pistol, and it clattered to the floor.

"My arm," Greg moaned. "You broke my arm."

"It just feels that way," Frank said as he picked up the pistol and unloaded it. "Your arm is only dislocated. But if you make any sudden moves, I'll start breaking bones you didn't know you had."

Joe ran out of the shuttle simulator and joined his brother. "I was just getting warmed up," he said with a smile. "A few more swings with that robotic arm and I could have knocked him into the bleachers." He looked down at Greg, huddled on the floor, clutching his arm. "You stepped out of the strike zone," he said in a scolding tone. "That's cheating."

Frank gave his brother a look and helped Greg to his feet. "It's over now," he said softly.

Greg looked at him, pleading with his eyes. "I didn't want to hurt anybody. I just wanted to *be* somebody."

"I know," Frank said. "But maybe you should have tried to be somebody else."

*   *   *

It had been a long day and it wasn't over yet. First the Hardys had to deal with the security guards who had been alerted by the gunshots. Then they had to explain everything all over again to the Huntsville police. Detective Walsh couldn't decide if he should be happy that he had one less case to worry about or mad that the two teenage brothers didn't turn out to be the culprits.

Frank and Joe managed to slip away before the detective had a chance to consider seriously the notion of arresting them for withholding information in a criminal investigation.

The Hardys' work at Space Academy didn't end with Greg Fontana's arrest. They still had one crucial task to complete, and they were up before the sun and ready to tackle it.

"All set back there?" Frank called out over his shoulder.

"I'm as ready as I'll ever be," Joe replied.

"Let's do it then," Frank said.

"Hold on a second," a firm voice broke in. Maria Galewski looked at Frank over the waist-high control panel that separated their seats. "I'm the shuttle commander. I'll tell mission control when we're ready."

From the seat next to Joe's at the back of the flight deck, Alice Culbert laughed. "That's the way, Maria. Don't let them forget who's in charge."

"We need to clear up a few things before we get started," Maria said.

"You're the boss," Joe responded.

"Everything happened so fast this morning," Maria said. "I wasn't expecting this last-minute assignment switch."

"We've spent the past week training to expect the unexpected," Frank said. "You were always the best-qualified person for the commander's job. Now you've got it."

Maria shook her head slowly. "This is all going to take a little time to sink in. Greg confessed to everything?"

Frank nodded. "All his hopes for a comeback were riding on this one movie. When he found out that he might lose the starring role, he got desperate. He started the fire in the dorm room and rigged the harness on the Zero 'G' Wall so that he could play hero and get a lot of press attention."

Joe picked up the story. "When we started checking into the accidents, Greg got nervous. He knew we suspected Swain, so he sabotaged the RMS unit and planted the soldering gun in Swain's office, hoping we'd find it. If we hadn't gone to Swain's office for evidence, Greg probably would have figured out some way to lead us there."

"The rewired circuit board and the soldering gun were enough evidence for the camp director," Frank said, "but not for us. We kept digging, and Greg kept worrying. The short circuit that fried the computer terminal in the control room was supposed to be a warning to scare us off the case."

"But it was *my* terminal that blew up," Maria pointed out.

"It was *supposed* to be Frank's terminal," Joe reminded her. "You switched seats right before we started the launch."

"What about the car bomb?" Alice asked. "That could have done a lot worse than just scare you. You're lucky you weren't killed."

"Greg barely knew what he was doing," Frank explained. "He wasn't exactly a professional bomb maker. I think he was more shocked by the force of the blast than we were."

"If you're all through yakking in there," a gruff voice crackled over the intercom, "would you mind checking your instruments for the final countdown? In case you've forgotten, we have a mission to complete. Or do you have more important plans?"

"He's back," Joe said in a deep announcer's voice. "And he's badder than ever. The leanest, meanest, roughest, toughest Space Academy instructor of them all. The one, the only, Steve Swain."

"Put a lid on it and get to work," Swain said brusquely.

"Gee, I'm so glad we solved this case and got a chance to spend some more quality time with that guy," Joe remarked. "He really sounds like he loves his work."

A low chuckle drifted over the intercom. "This is the part I love the best. I'm going to enjoy watching you guys squirm when you hit some of the routines I've programmed into your mission."

Joe leaned over and tapped his brother on the shoulder. "Call the police and tell them they have the wrong man. Maybe we can get Swain locked up until the mission is over."

Frank smiled. "Relax, Joe. After what we've been through this week, we can handle anything Swain throws at us."

"Are you ready to find out?" Maria asked.

Frank gave her the thumbs-up signal. "Go for it."

"Wait a second," Joe said. "Before we blast off, I have one important question."

All eyes on the flight deck turned to him.

A mischievous grin spread across Joe's face. "What's the in-flight movie? If it's anything starring Greg Fontana, I'm out of here."

Frank and Joe's next case:

Former astronaut Perry Housman has invited Frank and Joe to Tunisia for the hundredth anniversary of the International Explorers Guild. There they join some of the most intrepid young men and women in the world—trailblazers, mountain climbers, deep-sea divers. But of all the challenges the explorers face, none is more deadly than the killer now in their midst! Thor Sonderstrom, who controls the money that can make or break an expedition, has been poisoned. Determined to unmask the murderer, the Hardys soon find that the site of the celebration, an ancient fortress, has turned into a perilous palace of intrigue. In a world of shadowy secrets and venomous hatreds, danger and death lurk in the most unexpected places ... in *A Taste for Terror,* Case #94 in The Hardy Boys Casefiles™.

THE HARDY BOYS CASEFILES™